Adeline Street

ALSO BY CAROL LYNCH WILLIAMS

Kelly and Me

ADELINE STREET

Carol Lynch Williams

Delacorte Press

Published by
Delacorte Press
Bantam Doubleday Dell Publishing Group, Inc.
1540 Broadway
New York, New York 10036

Library of Congress Cataloging in Publication Data

Williams, Carol Lynch.
Adeline Street / Carol Lynch Williams.
p. cm.
Summary: Leah finds that it takes a long time to come to terms with
her sister's death.
Sequel to: Kelly and me.
ISBN 0-385-31075-7
[1. Death—Fiction.   2. Grief—Fiction.   3. Family life—Fiction.
4. Grandfathers—Fiction.   5. Florida—Fiction.]   I. Title.
PZ7.W65588Ad   1995
[Fic]—dc20   94-20292   CIP   AC

Manufactured in the United States of America

April 1995

10   9   8   7   6   5   4   3   2   1

BVG

*For Dad and Shirley and Aunt Linda and Kelly.
But most especially for Nana, who will
always live in my heart.*

November

THE YEAR'S BEGINNING

I just don't know if this sad and alone feeling will ever go away.

I mean, I feel like I could scream forever and not get out all the upset and afraid and sad that I have inside. But even if I screamed as big as the Grand Canyon, somehow I know that these awful feelings would still be here. And it scares me.

Some nights I jerk awake, cold and shaking, and I don't know why. Then I see Kelly's empty bed, the moonlight flowing over the neat covers. And like a bad dream I remember us getting ready to eat breakfast all over again. I almost smell the eggs cooking, almost hear Momma trying to talk us out of having Pop-Tarts. And then, like a picture that is always in my head, I can see my sister's face, Kelly's face, turning pale. And she's falling, falling out of her chair, slow to the floor, squeezing my hand tight, pulling me down to the ground with her. Then she is dead.

Papa, my grandfather, he still hurts because of Grammy's dying four years ago. They were married years and years. Longer than Kelly and I were best friends. Will I feel this way as long as Papa has about Grammy?

Or Mrs. Comer, who lives next door to us on Adeline Street. She's older than Papa by nearly ten years. Her husband has been dead since before I was born. And still she misses him. Will that happen to me?

Sometimes, before, when Kelly was alive, we would go over to Mrs. Comer's house to keep her company. She's afraid of lightning storms, and whenever there is one, and we have a lot here in Florida, she always has somebody come to her house and sit with her. I still do that now.

Last night the lightning was dancing everywhere in the distance, far out over the ocean. The sky was dark purple with thunderheads. To me there's hardly anything more scary or more beautiful than a lightning storm. I walked slow over to Mrs. Comer's house, pushing through the hibiscus hedge that separates our yards. The red flowers were starting to close up for the night.

I sat out on the porch for a little while, smelling the thick odor of the gardenia bushes that were planted all the way around the house, until Mrs. Comer's whiny voice dragged me in.

"Leah," she said, "you're going to be struck by lightning. A stray bolt is going to find you there, swinging in that old porch swing."

"That lightning is out by the ocean, Mrs. Comer," I said.

"That may be," she said through the screened window, "but storms travel fast. And lightning is sneaky. Once when I was a little girl, I heard of a man being hit by lightning when he was in Georgia and the storm was in North Carolina."

"That's not possible," I said, but I went into the living room, just in case.

I pushed the windows open and propped them up with pieces of wood. The wind moved the sheer curtains toward me, like an old-timey lady spinning in her ballroom dress. Then it sucked the curtains flat onto the screen.

Mrs. Comer sat hunched in her old rocker. She was wrapped in an orange, brown, and green afghan. After a moment I went through the house, unplugging every lamp, the television, the electric coffeepot, and on and on. Then I lit the kerosene lamp on top of the TV. Every once in a while thunder would rumble toward us, rolling like a big ball, and Mrs. Comer would shiver. The light from the lamp flickered, sending out a warm, soft glow.

Suddenly Mrs. Comer started remembering.

"When I was a little girl there were no cars. Horses and buggies were how we got around. Kerosene lamps were how we saw at night. No electric lights. Winters were never cold, and the only thing we had to worry about were the hurricanes that swept through. And then only in September." September was when Kelly died. Just two months before.

I settled myself on an old sofa and pulled my feet up under me. Some people, like Papa and my daddy, say that Mrs. Comer is senile. Momma thinks she's just old and lonely.

"I was the prettiest woman in all this area." I couldn't imagine that, what with all of Mrs. Comer's wrinkles. Was she ever really young? "Of course, there weren't all the towns and stores and golf courses and things that we have now. Mostly there were woods and palmettos brushes and flatlands going on and on forever. And orange groves, the trees heavy with fruit and thick, green, waxy leaves. White boxes of beehives. Beautiful herds of cows." I wondered if Mrs. Comer was all there right now or just being senile. How could anyone think herds of cows were beautiful?

"I miss all that open land. I miss all the lakes and the rivers flowing clean and pure. You know, I saw the beach on the television the other day and the water was dirty and ugly." She tsked her disapproval. From the backyard I could hear Mrs. Comer's crazy rooster crowing. I guess he thought it was late, what with the sky so dark.

"Yes sirree," Mrs. Comer said. "I was the belle of the ball." She leaned toward me, lifting her wrinkled hands from her lap, and for a moment I wondered if she might get up and whirl and dance with the curtains to prove that she really had been popular. I mean, it was possible for her to dance around without any warning.

"All of the young men wanted to be with me. My dance card was always full, but I only had eyes for Edward." Mrs. Comer was staring at the lamp, caught in the magic of its glow.

"He was the most handsome man alive." I felt sad, and I wasn't quite sure why. Maybe because I had sat in this room so many times with Kelly. Maybe because of Mrs. Comer's oldness.

"My mother didn't want me to marry Edward because he was fourteen years older than I was."

"Wow," I said.

"But I defied her." Mrs. Comer kept talking like she hadn't heard me. She gathered the afghan close around her shoulders like she was cold, even though the air was hot and heavy. Only the surges. of wind from the ocean were cool. I wondered what they did back in the olden days if you did something wrong like marry a man fourteen years older than you.

"In the middle of the night Edward came to the house and called for me, soft, under my window. I was already dressed. I tiptoed down the stairs and to the front door. Never had the stairs squeaked so." Mrs. Comer giggled. "I was so nervous. I thought I would wake the servants that Mother employed.

"Edward was waiting for me on the steps. I remember the smell of the gardenia bushes, and since that night I have loved that aroma best. He helped me up on his horse and jumped up behind me. Then we rode slowly away from the home of my youth. I didn't go back there until a year and a half later, with our first baby girl."

I couldn't believe the lady who had told Momma and Daddy about Kelly and me skinny-dipping would have left her own home without her mother's saying it was okay. My mouth dropped open. I mean, Mrs. Comer is one of the biggest snoops on Adeline Street, maybe even in all of New Smyrna Beach.

"Mother and Father welcomed me with open arms. And Edward too. They could see I was happy. More happy than I would ever be with another man."

For a while Mrs. Comer sat quiet, staring into the light of the kerosene lamp. Great jabs of lightning lit up the windows and showed the trees in the yard darkly, swaying and bending. Thunder boomed and rolled ever closer to us.

"Then he went to war," said Mrs. Comer. "And I thought I'd never see him again. But he came home, not a scratch, except maybe he was a bit thin. It didn't take long for me to fatten him up. Then he was gone again." Mrs. Comer let out a sad, deep sigh.

After a little bit her face softened as if her memories were good ones, and she said, "I expect him back any minute, you know, and when he gets here, you will have to run along home."

Outside, it was quiet for a brief moment. I could hear the porch swing, squeaking back and forth.

I went cold inside for a few seconds. "The storm is not anywhere near over," I said. "And you don't like to be alone during lightning storms."

Mrs. Comer smiled at me. "I'm not afraid of anything when Edward is here. Not even storms."

There was a creaking noise on the front porch, and Mrs. Comer leaped up and off the sofa. She squinted a look out the windows.

"Edward?" she said. "Edward, is that you?"

I got this scary feeling in my chest, and my heart started pounding hard.

"Finally you are back. Are you wanting to come in?" Mrs. Comer's voice was all shaky, and it sounded, well, excited and happy. "The door's open, Edward. I've been waiting for you for such a long time."

Mrs. Comer hurried to the door, stumbling over an ottoman. She was up in a flash, before I could even stand to help her. I watched openmouthed. This was the craziness that Papa and Daddy talked about. The afghan fell from around her shoulders and to the floor. Mrs. Comer left it where it landed. She flung the door wide open, and the curtains swooshed into the screens and strained to get past.

A moth flew a frenzied pattern to the kerosene lamp. The rooster crowed again, and I jumped. The wind belched in a burst of air that grabbed at Mrs. Comer's cotton dress and pulled it back into the house. The smell of the ocean swirled in.

"Edward?" Mrs. Comer said. It was a pitiful cry, sad and lonely. I went and stood beside her. She is tiny, just my height. Her hair is white really, but in the darkness of the night it looked silver in the front and gold in the back because of the lamplight. I put my arm around her. The heavens were split wide open then, with a bolt that divided the sky into a purple puzzle, shadowed dark and darker. We both saw the figure pushing through the hibiscus hedge.

"Edward!" Mrs. Comer called, her hands pressing against her lips. "Come home! Come home to me." She held her arms out suddenly to the approaching figure, waving him in with her hands.

"Mrs. Comer," I said, "that's just Papa, coming to check on us."

And then, as if the storm had brought me a truth, I saw Mrs. Comer as she really was: alone without her best friend. Like me without Kelly.

"Come in off the porch," I said. "It'll be raining soon and I don't want you to get wet."

"But if Edward is much later, his dinner will be cold."

"Mrs. Comer," I said, "Edward's not here. He died. Remember. He died a long time ago." Papa walked slow through the yard, stepping carefully in the dark.

"How about I make you some Postum?" I said.

The sky lightened again, and I saw Mrs. Comer's face crumple in an instant, then change back to the right-now present.

"He's dead?" she said. I felt her straighten a tiny bit. "I know that. Sometimes, though, I am lucky and I forget. Oh, how I loved that man." She said this to herself. "And after all this time I still miss him. I have an ache in me this big." Her hands moved to her chest. It didn't make much sense, but somehow I knew what she meant. "Edward, I love you. I'm coming to you as soon as I can," she called, and she kissed her hands and flung them out wide. Her voice seemed to poke a hole in the sky, and the rain began to pour down. We waited for Papa, then turned around together and went back inside.

We went to the cemetery in Edgewater, Momma and Daddy and Papa and I. Grandma and Uncle Wing followed in their car. Momma's sisters said they would stop by later. Today is November 26 and is Kelly's birthday. She would have been eleven if she hadn't died from the aneurysm. I sat in the car and watched my family trudge to where my sister is buried. I still cannot look at her grave. I don't know why.

I cried for a while. I felt angry for a while. I waited for them to come back, first watching and listening to a mockingbird sing and then watching as another storm began over the ocean, rolling up dark and sad.

Before they got back into the car, the lightning was playing tag over the water, which I knew was as gray as the sky itself, the waves capping with thick white foam.

Daddy drove us to Burger King for dinner; then we drove around the old fort, alongside the river. The wind came in, and Papa rolled down his window and let the sticky air into the car. I rested my head on his shoulder.

When we pulled into the driveway at home, the sky was almost black. The streetlights had flickered on and were glowing small orange moons of light down onto the road. I leaped out of the car and ran across the lawn to Mrs. Comer's. I squished through the hedge.

"Kelly, Kelly, Kelly" my feet seemed to say as I ran. I ached inside. Large, fat raindrops plopped around and on me.

When I got to her house, I was greeted by the heavy smell of gardenias and Mrs. Comer. She slung open the front door wide, and I went in to wait out the storm with her.

December

THE GIFT

After Kelly's birthday with no celebration, Momma, Daddy, Papa, and I spent nearly one whole week arguing whether or not to have Christmas. The weather refused to get Christmas cold. The leaves on the trees clung to the branches. Whenever the wind blew, it was as if they were chattering complaints that they were tired and ready to drop off. But it wasn't because of the weather that I didn't think we should have Christmas. It was because of Kelly.

Daddy and Papa both insisted that Kelly would want us to celebrate. That she would want us to have a tree, and hang stockings, and even have Momma and her sisters singing at the new Methodist church at the end of Adeline Street.

Just a month after Kelly was buried, a new church was built on the empty lot going toward the Sugar Mill. Not long after it was completed, Preacher Johnson came to our place and said he'd like for us to join his congregation. He knew all about us. He talked about Papa's maybe getting his driver's license back and asked if we would ever get another dog now that George Furd had been gone so long.

He even talked about Kelly, about her dying so suddenly. It was like he'd been peeping in our lives forever. I didn't much like it. Neither did Papa. Momma is always saying that I'm becoming more and more like my grandfather. Maybe that's because he's lived with us for so long now that part of him is starting to rub off on me.

Anyway, Momma and Daddy began frequenting the Methodist church. They told me they were going to this new place because it was close enough to walk, but I was really bothered by it. I mean, all my life we had been attending the big Baptist church downtown, and it just didn't seem right to change all of a sudden.

After a while Preacher Johnson asked Momma to sing with her sisters at this big ritzy dinner and program they wanted to put on at Christmas time. With Daddy and Papa prompting her, Momma decided to do it. And that was okay with me.

But Christmas Day would be a different story altogether. I felt as if we were being disloyal to Kelly. I like Christmas and all, but Kelly went wild over it. She just liked giving. She'd save all her money for months. She'd make gifts at school or sit in our walk-in closet, working on stuff for me and Momma and Daddy and Papa. She would hide the presents in secret places, all wrapped up. Then, when you were right in the middle of a good show on TV, she'd say, "I know what you're getting for Christmas," in a singsong voice. It used to irritate me. Now I wouldn't mind if she'd do it just one more time.

I'm just the opposite. Christmas Eve I'd go in and beg some money off Daddy or Papa, then run down to the Dollar Store to shop. It would always be crowded with last-minute shoppers and nearly empty of anything good.

I'd have to hunt for gifts. A hot pink bra for Momma, because that would be the only color left, or maybe even a candy dish. She collects them. Socks, slightly imperfect, for Daddy. An old book on men's grooming for Papa. I'd search for something good for Kelly, but like I said, pickings just aren't that terrific Christmas Eve. The dolls always have one blinking eye that gets stuck, and my sister never really liked dolls that much. The dogs that you set in the back of your car, the ones that nod their heads, have rhinestones missing from their collars. The mirrors in the brush and comb sets are warped.

Last year I got Kelly two boxes of Life Savers, the kind that look like books, because they are her favorite, and a sweatshirt with a tiger painted on it. It had one big black jewel for the right eye and a glob of glue for the left. It was also a little too big. X-X-L. I picked the one good eye off so that it wouldn't look too funny, then wrapped it up in newspaper.

I remember Kelly ranted and raved about it, even though it hung gap-necked and huge on her. She slept in it every night till April and it was just too hot to wear anymore. She would have probably kept on wearing it and sweating in it, but I finally told her just to sleep in her underwear till it got cold again. Now the shirt is folded in the third drawer of her dresser.

I was outvoted three to one on celebrating. Papa and I were in the sunroom, and he was sitting in Daddy's favorite chair. I think Papa's adopted it for his very own. Daddy doesn't seem to mind too much. In fact, it doesn't seem that much of anything bothers us anymore. It's like we're all just plodding away at life.

"Papa," I said, "I don't think we're being fair here. Fair to Kelly. She's the one that really loved Christmas." We had already had our Christmas discussion and Momma and Daddy had decided that we were going to have gifts and a tree. I had argued no. Now I was mad. And since Papa had sat pretty silent during the decision-making time, I decided to talk to him about it.

Papa looked hard at me.

"What do you think we should do?" he said.

"Cancel it," I said.

"You can't cancel Christmas," Papa said.

"They do it all the time in books."

Papa didn't say anything. He's real good about that. I mean, if I'm having a hard time worrying over all that's happened, he just sits and listens.

Maybe because he remembers the hurting he felt when his baby boy died, and then his wife, Grammy.

"If my life was a book," I said, "I'd tear out the ending. I'd rewrite it. Kelly would be alive and it would be Christmas every day." Tears welled up in my eyes. "And then I'd study it out, every time, till I knew exactly what she wanted, the way she always did for me. And I'd buy that thing, maybe two or three of that thing, and then wrap it up in the shiniest paper I could find. Not in crummy old newspaper. Newspaper is for wrapping fish. And I'd even buy one of those expensive bows and glue one to each gift I gave her." My voice was squeaky and all stretched out.

"Come here, Leah," Papa said, holding his arms out to me. I walked over to Papa and climbed up in his lap. I folded my feet up so they wouldn't touch the floor. Papa has always said that I could sit on his lap as long as my feet don't touch the ground. I buried my head into his neck and sniffed his aftershave.

"There now," he said. It seemed both sad and funny for Papa to be saying something like that, and I thought I might laugh. Instead, I started crying. It was like a wail, and reminded me of when George Furd, Papa's favorite dog, had been alive and tied up to the doghouse in the backyard near the garage. He would always throw his head back and howl his unhappiness at the disgrace of being tied there.

"Christmas is gonna keep on coming," he said. He squeezed me up close, and I sobbed.

But after a while I made up my mind to celebrate Christmas.

All week long I thought of gifts for my family. I went into the walk-in closet in my room and worked on surprises for Momma and Daddy. I sat in the dark, probably exactly like Kelly had, hidden in the church dresses that hung down, cool and wispy.

I lay in bed late at night, unable to sleep, thinking about what I could get Papa. He was the tough one to give to. Not that he ever minded getting old-fashioned grooming books or those funny glass birds that are filled with colored water and rock and dip. But I wanted him to have something as good as last year's gift.

Kelly came up with this idea to give Papa a cassette tape with all of his favorite songs taken from his country and western records, so that he could listen to his music in the car. Months later the three of us were listening to that very tape when Papa got in a wreck, then had his license revoked for leaving the scene of an accident. Anyway, it took us a couple of hours to get that done. We had to wait for him to go off to the VFW or fishing or something to work on it. It had been fun sneaking around, planning, preparing.

And when Papa opened that gift up and started listening to the tape, he just laughed and laughed. I guess because we had introduced each of the songs and even sung in a couple of places, yodeling and harmonizing whenever the country spirit struck. Kelly and I got a big kick out of watching Papa.

After a long while of thinking, I decided that I'd write Papa a poem and a letter for being so good to me.

I wondered if maybe this jittery, warm, Jell-O feeling was the way Kelly felt when she planned. I was doing this special gift giving for Kelly. I mean, since Christmas and giving gifts and doing all that planning meant so much to her, maybe if I did all this, we would feel a little like we had Kelly for the day.

Christmas Eve Momma came to me and asked if I wanted to go shopping with her.

"No, thanks, Momma," I said. I was feeling really sad, thinking of the lonely next day to come. "I've gotten all my stuff already."

Momma's eyebrows went up. She has never liked it that I don't take that much time in picking out gifts. She and Kelly are a lot the same that way, taking their time to find the exact right thing. I always thought that when Kelly grew up she'd be the spitting image of Momma, having the same long blond hair and sprinkle of freckles.

Then I remembered. I wasn't done shopping. Here I'd thought and thought, trying to make everything right, trying to pick out the perfect thing for

Momma and Daddy and Papa, and I'd left out the most important person there was.

"Yeah," I said. "I'll go."

The weather was hardly cold enough for even a sweater. It was dark out though. The moon was a tiny slice, just edging its way up, and the stars were hard to see. Along the road the trees were dark, like the black shadows in a painting. The stores would be closing in less than an hour.

We drove past the Methodist church, where the preacher was just locking up. He waved when Momma beeped but never even turned around to see who it was.

A single cross glowed on top of the church. In the side yard there was a live manger scene. People from the congregation volunteered for two-hour shifts and kept the scene going both night and day. I looked at it as we drove past.

There was Mary looking down at a baby doll Jesus. Joseph stood next to her, and they both peered at the doll or off into the distance, past the bright lights that shone on them. A couple of shepherds wandered around with two real sheep. A cow was tied to a post right outside the makeshift shed.

Momma would be singing tomorrow with her sisters about the very thing I was looking at: a baby being born in a stable. I'd heard them practice for days now, polishing the words and harmonies. The tune came into my mind, and I hummed it.

Momma wanted to go to Wal-Mart, so we drove down that way. People's houses were decorated with lights and fake Santa Clauses and Season's Greetings signs of red, white, and green. I bet we were the only family in all New Smyrna that didn't have up outdoor decorations. We'd only gotten a tree four days earlier. It took another whole day for us to get the lights and ornaments on. When we started working on it, though, all of us, Papa, Momma and Daddy, and even me, we started remembering other Christmases, and it was fun.

Wal-Mart is in the new section of town, just a couple of blocks from Main Street where I usually do my last-minute Christmas shopping. I walked around with Momma until she finally told me to let her be.

"I can't buy anything for you if you're standing right here under my arm," she said. "Why don't we meet at the front doors at closing time?"

I smiled at Momma, and she swatted at me. Her hair was hanging a little loose from when she'd swept it up off her face before we left. She looked sad and tired. I put my arms around her small waist and hugged her tight. She rested her chin on my head. I could smell White Shoulders cologne, soft and subtle. It was kind of funny to me that she wouldn't already have gotten everyone something. She was starting to be like me maybe.

I wandered around the store for a while. Clear-

23

ance signs were everywhere. Bright red with green plastic bells hanging from them. The store lights were harsh. I walked past a mirror and was surprised at how I looked. My hair seemed a lot redder than usual, probably because of the lights. It was hanging straggly and a little wiry. My freckles were poking out. I still had some of my summer tan, but it looked funny, kind of washed out. Every day I had been looking at myself in the mirror, but I had never noticed how sad I looked until right then.

Nothing was right in Wal-mart. Maybe because I was lonesome for last year.

Then it hit me. I was only a few blocks from the Dollar Store. Any other year I could do my shopping in a record thirty minutes there. Why not now? I ran out the door and started jogging toward Main. A cool breeze pushed my hair back and snapped my shirt. I ran past the bank. The sign said 63 DEGREES and 6:18 P.M. HAPPY HOLIDAYS TO YOU AND YOURS. I jogged around the corner, under the magnolia trees that lined the sidewalks. Each was dressed in tiny white lights that twinkled like fireflies, off, then on, then off, then on again.

Now I was back in the older part of town, my favorite place in New Smyrna. A homesick feeling welled up into my throat, but I swallowed it. I could slow down now. Here the trees were oak and huge, spreading across the street, their branches sometimes meeting in the middle with the oaks from the opposite side of the road. In the summer driving through this part of town can make you feel like you are in a cave. Now large red candles swung suspended across the street by wires that were wrapped in green foil.

I breathed deep, and the cool air seemed to settle me. I walked past Anita's Nail Salon, where a huge hand with long, painted nails decorated the window. Next was the Rexall drugstore. A tired-looking man was locking up the front doors. He smiled and waved at me and mouthed "Merry Christmas." I waved back. A few steps more and I was at the Dollar Store.

The door buzzed when I entered, and the lady behind the register looked up at me. She didn't look especially happy, and I didn't blame her. Here it was nearly closing time on Christmas Eve, and another customer had just walked in the door.

I walked down the aisles of cellophane-wrapped toys from Taiwan. I picked up a doll. Yep, one eye would not open. She winked on and on at me. There was something comfortable knowing that things were still the same here.

I went past the slightly imperfect socks and the toothpaste and the shampoos. There was a big table of tennis shoes, mostly left ones, that smelled all rubbery. Makeup wasn't right. Neither was a wig. Now, even though I was a few feet from the perfume aisle, I could smell all the different, cheap brands. A lady's voice came over the intercom announcing that the Dollar Store would be closing in five minutes and that all customers should bring their purchases to the check out stand.

I was just about to give up when I saw the candy table. Everything was priced half. That is one good thing about the Dollar Store. They do have pretty good sales. I found what I wanted there and headed to pay. The lights flicked once, twice, three times, then finally went out in the back half of the store, and the Christmas music quit playing with a squeak. I stopped next to the candy dish aisle. There was a real shiny silver one shaped like a big frog. His mouth was open wide so you could put your hand in there and get the candy out. I thought about Momma for a second and then decided no. I already made her and Daddy a scrapbook collection of things Kelly had written and colored and drawn the past summer.

There was a long line at the checkout. Right in front of me was an old man. He was a little stooped over and he had on a plaid jacket that hung way down on his shoulders. The leather elbow pads were coming unsewn. He was holding a box of butter mints and one of the candy-dish frogs. His hair was yellow from age, and he had brushed it back neatly. I started feeling sad.

The lady at the register was plenty irritated. She grumbled with each customer. Finally the old man stood in front of her. She rang up his purchases, then tapped her long red nails impatiently as he took out a small change purse and began to count money. I wondered if she got her nails done at Anita's Nail Salon. There was a small Christmas tree glued to the top of one nail, and I just couldn't see how she could have put it on herself and not messed up all that red paint. I was thinking how could she do anything with nails that long when I heard her say, "You ain't got enough here. You're eight cents short." Her fingers stopped tapping.

I looked at the old man. His face started to color. I noticed a stubble of beard, all white. Nothing like Papa's, which has a tinge of red when he allows it to grow.

"I thought with the candy being half price I could get both," he said, and he reached into his pockets, looking for the change. His hands came out empty.

"I hate it when old people think they can come into this store and not have enough money for what they are trying to buy. Don't you know if this register is short, it comes out of my pocket?" The clerk jabbed herself in the chest with a long nail, then snapped her gum in disgust.

The old man bowed his head in shame. "I guess I'll put one of these back," he said. He touched the frog gently with two fingers, trying to make the decision.

"This is for my wife," he said softly, first to the

girl, who rolled her eyes at him, and then to me. I nodded, unable to move. He picked up the mints. "I guess I'll just put this back," he said; only this time his voice was softer. He turned and moved back to the candy table.

"It just makes me sick to see people like that. Always trying to take advantage of others," the girl said. I looked at her tight white face. Her lips were pinched together. Her eyes were covered with dark blue eye shadow. My stomach started to hurt. The old man was back now.

"Check it out first next time," she said. "Save yourself and everyone else some embarrassment." She handed the man his bag with the silver frog in it and his change, and he walked out. The door buzzed angrily till it clicked shut.

I looked at the girl with amazement.

"Shut your mouth," she said, entering the prices of my two items. "I bet he's filthy rich. He's probably climbing into his brand-new Cadillac right now." I continued to stare at her.

So this was Christmas, I thought. People like this lived, and would probably live forever, and my sister was dead. Dead without a warning. I let my mouth hang open wider and kept looking at the girl, even when she handed me my bag.

"Get out of here, you little brat," she said. And turned her back on me.

"Merry Christmas," I said at the door. I wanted to spit to get the nasty taste out of my mouth.

Outside, the wind blew cool into my face. It seemed maybe the weather might turn Christmasy after all. I looked down the street. The old man was just turning the corner.

"Hey," I said, only it was too soft to hear. "Hey!"

I started running after the old man. My package thumped in my hand. "Wait," I called. But he had already disappeared from me. My feet smacked the sidewalk as I ran to catch him. I stumbled over a raised section of sidewalk but righted myself without falling. I had to catch up to that man! I had to.

I turned the corner, and he was there, opening the door to his car. It was an old blue Ford.

"Hey," I said. He looked over at me. I was winded, even though I had run only a short distance and my heart was thumping loudly. "I have something for you. For your candy dish." I opened my bag and pulled out a box of Life Savers.

The old man shook his head. "I can't take those," he said. "You've bought them for somebody else."

"Yes," I said. "They're for my sister. I bought them for my sister. But she's dead." I stopped, thinking how crazy it must sound, but the old man just looked at me with a steady and sad gaze. I hurried on. "And if she were here, I know she'd want me to give them to you. Please," I said. "Please take them. I have another one." I raised the bag.

The old man took the candy from me. Then he leaned forward and kissed the top of my head.

I turned and ran toward Wal-Mart. I was late.

At home, after everyone was in bed, I went over to Kelly's dresser. I opened her drawer and put the second box of Life Savers on the tiger sweatshirt.

Then I went back to bed and finally to sleep.

January

THE PREACHER

Christmas was okay. Lots of people showed up or stopped by, I guess to check on us. People from the church down the road and the Baptist church near the river sent so much food that we had to freeze some. After dinner Daddy's momma, Grandma, and his brother, Uncle Wing, came over and washed the dishes for us.

The first week in January Preacher Johnson came for a visit. He brought a really big fruit basket that he said was to the Orton family from the entire congregation. I couldn't help thinking that that meant Momma and Daddy must have somehow contributed to the gift to themselves. The bananas were green, even under the pink cellophane.

"I've got a little message for you," he said, after Momma, Daddy, Papa, and I sat down. It was all about praying and how that will help the weary and sad soul. He talked about death not really being a sad thing but a stage in life, and how Kelly was sitting, right that very moment, next to God. It went on and on. I thought sure the preacher was going to pass a collection plate around if he ever finished yacking. Pretty soon it started to bug me. I mean, here we were, a family trying to forget things, and he was standing there reminding us.

I just looked at him. I was sitting on the sofa, stretched out as big as I could be. So was Papa. Our heads met at the middle. Somehow Papa and I had managed to take up the whole thing. I draped one of my legs casually over a sofa arm. Neither one of us wanted Preacher Johnson sitting with us. It was an unspoken thing. The preacher kept on looking expectantly at me.

Then he started talking about how prayer was a real miracle.

Suddenly I was so mad I could have spit nails. "Ha!" I said.

"Excuse me?" said the preacher. His dark eyebrows arched high onto his forehead.

Momma cleared her voice and shook her head at me real slow because she didn't want me to say anything, but she didn't want the preacher noticing her having to tell me to behave either.

"I said ha!" I said again.

"Honey," Daddy said. "Leah," and his tone made me really sad because I could see how bad he was feeling. Sometimes I forget that I'm not the only one who lost Kelly.

"Let her talk," said Papa.

"Yes," said the preacher, "let her speak. Perhaps I can help to ease her of this heavy burden she carries." He gave me this half-smile that showed just a bit of his very straight and very white teeth. His eyes were blue like ice. He looked like he felt he knew all the answers to life's questions. I clenched and unclenched my fists.

"You can't ease my mind and neither can your prayers," I said. I sat up. It was suddenly very quiet in the room. I could hear the grandfather clock in the hall winding up to chime.

"We said prayers from the moment Kelly fell on the floor over there"—I jerked my head toward the dining room—"till the moment the doctor came out to tell us there was nothing they could do for her, and didn't nothing help." I was sitting up real straight now.

"If prayers work miracles," I said, "then why is Kelly dead?"

"It was just the will of our loving God."

I rolled my eyes toward the ceiling. "Puh-lease," I said. "If God is really a loving God, then why isn't Kelly here?" My voice was starting to get loud. I thought I might start crying, and that made me madder still.

"God cannot be mocked," said the preacher, standing up. He was angry now. I stood too, and so did Papa. "We don't question Him."

"Ha!" I said between clenched teeth. The preacher towered above me. "You're wrong. If there's a loving God like you say, then we can ask Him anything." Then I got real quiet, because suddenly I knew what was wrong. This man just did not know what to tell me.

"You don't have any answers," I said, my voice tired. "You don't know anything. Don't blame God, saying He took Kelly away. Blame yourself because you don't have the answers."

Papa started a slow, hard clapping, and the preacher, his face bright red, moved to let himself out of the house.

"I'll pray for you," he said to me. It almost sounded like a threat. The door clicked shut behind him.

Strange as it was, that was the best I felt since Kelly died. The heavy grudge and anger that I'd had against the Heavenly Father were finally gone.

February

FISHING

It was early Sunday morning when Uncle Wing rang the bell. Papa ran tiptoeing to the front door and threw it wide open. I whispered hello from across the room. I was going fishing with the two of them, not to church. Momma wasn't really happy about that, but she was letting me decide.

"Shhhh!" Papa said, in the loudest whisper I ever heard. "You're gonna wake the entire house." Papa tiptoed back to where I sat in the dining room. Uncle Wing clumped through the living room, his big black fishing boots announcing his arrival. He let the screen door slam behind him.

"Andy ain't awake?" he said. It was five forty-five.

"He wasn't before you got here," Papa said, sitting down with me.

Uncle Wing grinned big. "The truck's ready to go," he said. "Except for your fishing gear." He was dressed like a sloppy ol' fisherman in paint-stained army fatigues and a big holey sweatshirt that was gnarled at the neck. His hat was decorated with an assortment of fishhooks, a couple that had dried bait left on them. Uncle Wing believes in conserving space, I guess because his boat is so small, so he either wears his gear or carries it all in one hand.

"Won't take but a second to throw that in the back," said Papa. He was worrying this way and that, packing last-minute things in the picnic basket.

"I've got an ice chest full of beer out there calling my name," said Uncle Wing. Then he winked at me. "Leah, can you wait?" he said. "Can you hardly wait? Fishing at the end of February. Who'd a thunk it?"

Right after a really cold spell in January the weather changed to nearly summer temperatures. At least it felt that way. Every day it was at least eighty degrees.

"Craziest thing I have ever seen," Daddy said once while watching the country weather reporter on Channel 2. "Look, it's snowing by the buckets in Utah and so hot here you could get a sunburn if you were out five minutes."

When the forecaster said that we wouldn't be sweating too much longer, Papa called Uncle Wing and they decided to go fishing on the river just to say they had.

Uncle Wing belched and scratched under his arm. Then he jumped up from the table and got two coffee cups. He poured them full from the pot that Papa had already made and set one cup in front of me.

"Drink this here coffee," said Uncle Wing. "You

don't want to miss a single minute of your grampa's and my magnificent fishing." Uncle Wing leaned toward me. He sure did look a lot like my daddy. Not his hair. Daddy is more of a redhead, and Uncle Wing has brown hair. But his blue eyes, and even the smile creases around them, looked like Daddy.

"I got a secret-ingredient bait in-tensifier that drives fish absolutely crazy," said Uncle Wing. "I invented it myself, and I'm thinking of getting a patent on it." He winked at me, and I wasn't sure whether he was kidding or not.

See, Uncle Wing has invented quite a few things, and according to Daddy, he is set for life. It bugs Daddy to no end that Uncle Wing won't do more than one inventing project every once in a while, and the rest of the time he just plays and takes care of Grandma. Daddy says if he had a brain like his brother's, he would spend five years inventing things and the rest of his life on vacation. He says we'd be living high off the hog for an absolute eternity.

To look at Uncle Wing, you'd think you'd need to loan him money for a cup of coffee. Style isn't important to him. He wears any old thing. He lets his hair get shaggy. He needs to exercise. His shoes always look like the laces are holding them together. And by the way, if you did offer him coffee money, he'd take it. He's just like that.

Uncle Wing started poking through the picnic basket.

"By the time we get home this afternoon, our ice chest is gonna be empty of beer and full of fish," he said. "We may even need this to put extra fish in." He thumped the basket with his finger. "We're gonna be eating good tonight." Uncle Wing whooped. Papa hushed him.

"Keep it down," Daddy hollered from upstairs. I could tell he was irritated.

"Grump," Uncle Wing said, grinning.

I poured sugar and canned milk into my coffee, then sniffed deep. Coffee sure does smell good. But it's one of the worst things that I have ever tasted in my life. I slurped it up, because Uncle Wing thought I should. Yep, no matter what you put in coffee, it never tastes good. I added more sugar and more milk. Finally it was gone. At the bottom of my cup grounds swirled. Some got into my mouth and I spit them back. Papa put two egg sandwiches in front of me and I started eating them. It's bad luck to fish on an empty stomach.

"Reached your fortune?" Uncle Wing said, grabbing my coffee cup. "By dang, girl, it says we're gonna have us one helluva day fishing. And what's this? Something's gonna happen to you what's never happened before!" I laughed with him and Papa, happy for the moment.

"Shhh!" I said. "Daddy and Momma." I was

starting to get excited. I gulped my food, then wiped my mouth with a napkin. It was time to go.

We tiptoed to the door.

"Night, Andy," Uncle Wing called to my father, letting the screen door slam behind him.

We walked out to Uncle Wing's old Chevy truck. His small boat was hooked up behind. We threw our poles and the rest of our gear onto the floor of the boat.

"We got everything?" Papa said. We all were peering hard at the stuff that only looked like a lump of blackness, straining to make our eyes see. It wasn't quite morning yet.

"Sure do," said Uncle Wing, slamming his hand on the bow of the boat. "Let's get this show on the road." We all piled into the cab of the truck. I was squished in the middle.

Uncle Wing's truck is so old it smells like ancient plastic. A tiny crack separates the windshield into two parts: one for Uncle Wing, the other for his passenger.

The truck started with a blast. As we pulled out of the driveway, it backfired, making me jump.

"Ha-ha!" said Uncle Wing. "If you two only had an older brother." He pounded his fist against the steering wheel, laughing. "I couldn't have planned that one better myself." I felt a little stab in my chest. I had had a younger sister. The light in Momma and Daddy's upstairs room flicked on as we roared out of the driveway and down to the stop sign, where we turned left and headed for the river. "I bet your Daddy is wishing he'd never moved Momma and me here," Uncle Wing said to me, his shoulders still shaking. I don't know if Uncle Wing is right or not. Every once and a while I do hear Daddy grumbling what a hassle it is to have his brother so close, but I think he's really glad that he helped them get here last summer. Grandma's dying spells have decreased to nothing.

New Smyrna Beach, Florida, is the prettiest town I know. And I've traveled too. I've been to Panama City and Ocala and Gainesville and Eustis and St. Augustine, and, of course, Orlando. And all the little towns in between. St. Augustine runs a real close second to being as pretty as New Smyrna, but that's because of the old fort and shops and things. Not too many people know this, but New Smyrna's really the oldest city in the United States, and not St. Augustine. We have a fort, too, right near the Baptist church I go to, but it's in ruins. Since our little town could never be the tourist attraction that St. Augustine is, it's just kept quiet which town is the oldest. I guess that's okay. There's a few of us that know the real truth.

Anyway, New Smyrna is really beautiful. Especially the older section and especially in the early morning. The sun wasn't up yet, but on its way. The sky was starting to turn to warm colors. The dark houses and trees became more visible. We drove past the community park, where once I sat on Daddy's lap while he swung so high I thought I'd be able touch the leaves of the surrounding oak trees with my feet. There was no one there this early in the morning. We drove past the Red and White grocery. Papa reached over me and beeped at Jesse Norman, the store owner. He was just opening up, getting ready for business. He waved and shouted out Papa's name.

We traveled down Main, slow, past the drugstore and the Dollar Store. We went past the Ace hardware store and past the blue and white sign with an *H* on it that meant the hospital was at the end of that street.

We passed the tennis courts and the racquetball courts, and then far above the huge oak trees there was the water tower. I could just barely see the outline of the large star that sat on top. Each year at Christmastime, the city lights that star to remind everyone of the star in Bethlehem. I've always loved seeing it shine, high over everything, like it's sending a real important message.

On the right we passed the First Baptist Church, which my whole family used to go to, except Papa, of course. That was before the Methodist church was built.

I've decided I'm not going to the new church. Ever. I don't know why. Maybe there are just too many good memories tied up in this huge old brick place.

Like, I can remember my grandmother, Grammy, watching me and a bunch of other little kids in the nursery. I can remember putting pennies in a tin cup, one for each year of my life, at birthday time. I can remember, once, when it was time to go home, and Kelly was really excited to be out of church. She wasn't very old, maybe five or six. And she came running out of her Sunday school class, whooping and hollering, not even looking where she was going. She ran smack into the brick wall. There was blood everywhere, all down the front of her blue, white, and green dress, and it was dripping onto the floor, splatting like big red quarters. The wrinkled, old Sunday school teachers were running around like a bunch of cackling hens scared by a dog. Kelly sat down to bleed, and I ran and found Grammy. She put this really big bandage on the gash and sang songs to Kelly till Momma and Daddy came running up. Then we went over to Fish Memorial Hospital, and Kelly got seven black stitches. Later, looking at Kelly's little pink scar, we decided that Sunday had been a pretty good one. Kelly drew a thin red line on my forehead with a ballpoint pen, and we walked around the neighborhood, grinning.

At the church Uncle Wing turned right. There was the library, which is built in front of the river. This road is what Papa says is full of old money. The

houses here are huge and beautiful. There's lots of
neatly groomed grounds, edged in giant hibiscus
bush hedges. People here, Papa says, are rich because their great-great-great-grandpappy was rich.
I don't know about that. But with the sun coming up
fresh on these places, sparkling on the dew, it kind
of looked as if nothing could go wrong anymore.
That there was nothing really wrong right then. But
I knew better.

Papa swore Uncle Wing to secrecy and then
pointed out what he said was the best fishing place
on the entire river. Uncle Wing said an old mudhole
would be good enough for him. He had his secret
bait intensifier. Then he backed his boat into the
water. After parking the truck, he waded out to
where we were and climbed in with us.

The water slapped at the boat, and that was the
only sound in the early morning. It seemed that we
were the first up for the day. Then Uncle Wing
started the motor, which coughed out blue smoke.
We backed slowly into the river, and cruised against
the current until we came to the secret place Papa
had pointed out from the road. Uncle Wing threw
out the cinder-block anchor. Our fishing day had
begun.

There were only two things to sit on in Uncle
Wing's boat: a small board he had hammered up in
the front and a folding chair he sat on in the back. I
was pushing things this way and that, trying to find

a comfortable place in all the stuff that we had brought. There were our three fishing poles, a huge ice chest, the picnic basket. Four books that I had brought along in case I got bored of sitting. Two orange life jackets nearly bleached white from the sun. The secret bait intensifier and a bucket of bait, a pillow that I decided to sit on, and a little bit of rusty-looking water that sloshed around right where I was. My holey blue jeans were already wet, but as anyone knows, that's part of fishing.

"Gimme a beer," Uncle Wing said, first thing. He was digging through the bait bucket, looking for a fat worm. I handed him a beer from the ice chest. With one hand he popped open the can and with the other he stuck his worm first into the bait intensifier and then onto the hook at the end of his line. I looked away. Uncle Wing's intensifier looked like thick blue paint. It smelled like old garbage.

Fishing has always been one of my favorite things to do with Papa. Kelly and I used to go with him all the time. Sometimes we'd go to the little pond out in the woods behind our house. Once in a while we'd fish off the bridge that takes you to the beach. We'd fish off the jetty and, of course, right here where we were this morning. A couple of times we even went deep-sea fishing. All those times and never once did I have trouble baiting a hook. Papa's always been proud that I could do that.

But today. Today was different. All I could think

of was did it hurt the worm. That was something Kelly always worried about. Now it seemed to be stuck in my mind. Maybe all those times Kelly had felt sorry for the worms, maybe all those times she had been right. I decided I could not think about it. I looked over the side of the boat and into the dark water, past my white reflection and into the murkiness. I could see little bits of debris being carried away down this saltwater river. Everything was traveling with the current from the ocean.

"Here," Papa said, passing me my most lucky and favorite cane pole. I looked up at him. The sun broke the horizon. Now the rays were streaming bright past Papa and into my eyes. His body broke the white light, and I could see his outline perfectly. Papa's hair looked blond again, and for a second he seemed really young, like he is in his and Grammy's photo albums. Then the sun was up a little higher and shining directly in my face. I shielded my eyes from the light.

"You do it for me, Papa," I said. "I can't."

"You're missing the day," Uncle Wing said. He had already cast twice. He was reeling in his line slowlike. "Temptin' 'em," he said, and winked at me.

"You've never been squeamish before," Papa said.

"I know," I said. "I don't know what's wrong with me. I just can't do it."

"Never say can't," Uncle Wing said, " 'cause can't

never did nothin'," and he cast his line again into the river.

Papa took a worm from the bait bucket, dipped it, and threaded it on my hook. It wriggled and turned and twisted. The tip of its brown body, drenched in blue, searched the air for freedom. I looked at Uncle Wing so I didn't have to see the worm.

"You'll catch something good with that lively ol' thing for sure," Uncle Wing said. "A good worm and secret bait intensifier. That's all we'll be needing today. That and this beer." He touched the ice chest with the toe of his big black boot.

When I heard the worm plop into the water, I looked back at Papa. He was watching me close. I grinned at him. "The worst is over," I said. "I'll be okay from here on out." Papa smiled back.

Uncle Wing's bait was magic. He and Papa pulled up one fish after another. The fishing was so good for them that they threw anything back that weighed less than two pounds.

Each fish was threaded onto a stringer. Uncle Wing or Papa would stick the long metal clip through the fish's mouth, then out through its gill. Then they'd toss it back into the water to swim around. This way each one could be killed and eaten fresh.

I sat for more than two hours without a single bite. When I finally pulled up my line, I saw that my worm was gone. I hadn't had even a nibble so I knew the worm had probably worked its way off my hook. I was a little relieved. I wound the line around the cane pole and pulled out *The Borrowers Afloat*.

I'd read only a few pages when Uncle Wing said, "Come on, Leah! You ain't never gonna catch nothin' with your nose stuck in that book. Here. Try it one more time." And before I could say anything, he'd baited my hook and tossed it in the water.

Another long half hour passed. It was almost ten in the morning and nothing was happening except it was starting to get hot and I was starting to feel pretty sleepy. I took off my windbreaker and pulled an old blue baseball cap onto my head. The band pushed my bangs into my eyes.

I was just ready to pull my book out again when I felt a tug. I sat up straight. The line pulled stiff and taut. It sliced the water in half. I felt the fish struggle and fight far away from me, under the water.

"Hold her, Leah!" Papa said.

Uncle Wing whooped and stood up. The boat rocked from side to side.

I grinned with pleasure from seeing them so happy.

"This isn't so bad," I said aloud.

"Bad?" said Uncle Wing. "Bad? This is better than anything money can buy. We're all here to-gether and the sun's warm and we're fishing. What could be better than that? Huh, Papa? What could be better than that?"

"Not a lot," Papa said. And he laughed.

The sun warmed up the water. The river looked soft and smooth. On the bank across the way an egret took off, flapping its wings with a *wuh, wuh, wuh* whisper. I thought briefly about the Save the Egret campaign we had done recently in school.

"Well, will you look at this?" said Uncle Wing. He was holding the end of my line where a flat fish swung back and forth like a pendulum. It flapped and struggled. "Why, you've caught yourself a flounder, Leah. A flounder in this old saltwater river. Who'd a thunk it?" Then he laughed. "No wonder you weren't getting no bites. Your bait musta been restin' on the bottom of the river."

I looked at the fish wrestling to free itself from Uncle Wing, who was taking the hook out of its mouth and getting ready to put it on the stringer.

"Both of the eyes are on one side of its body," I said.

" 'Cause he lays flat on the bottom of the ocean," Papa said. He smacked his lips. "Them fish is good eatin'."

The flounder stared at me, both eyes. Its mouth opened and closed and opened and closed. The gills worked, trying to breathe the warm air. Uncle Wing threaded the flounder onto the metal stay with the other fish, then tossed them all into the river again. I could see the bellies of all the fish as they swam, slower and slower down to the end of the chain that kept them secured to the boat. Every once in a while one of their bellies would catch the sun and show up white, like a pale light in the murky water.

"Hot damn," Papa said. "What a cap for the morning. It's time for a nap." Papa reached into the ice chest and pulled himself out a beer. He snapped it open, grabbed a faded life preserver to lean on, and stretched out nearly the length of the boat. "Don't know why you even bother putting a motor on this tiny thing, Wing," he said. "We could paddle this just as fast with our hands."

Uncle Wing laughed. "I love appreciation," he said. He nudged at Papa's leg with the toe of his shoe. "Scootch over, Papa. I'm coming down there with you. This boat is big enough for our country's navy and you're taking up all the room. Hon, you can sit in the hot seat," Uncle Wing said, motioning to his chair. "I'm gonna rest with your grandfather if'n he moves hisself over."

"I'm an old man," Papa said. "I need to be able to unlax. That means I need lots of room." Papa closed his eyes.

"Old man, nothing," Uncle Wing muttered. He closed his eyes too. In a few minutes they both were sound asleep. Papa's hands held lightly to the beer. It rested on his belly and rose and fell with his breathing.

"I need a camera," I said, but neither of them moved. I was wedged between them, and my legs were starting to hurt. I got my book and moved into Uncle Wing's folding chair. I read for a while, then decided to see what Momma had packed for us the night before.

As soon as I opened the basket, I was hungry. Momma's chicken was a beautiful golden brown. The corn bread was perfect. In the center of each yellow square was a little pat of butter. I ate two pieces of chicken, a leg and a breast, and three good-size chunks of corn bread. Then I was thirsty.

I leaned over to the ice chest. There was one good thing about Uncle Wing's boat's being so small. From his folding chair he could reach nearly everything with just a little stretch.

Papa was snoring and smiling.

"Fishing's not so bad," I said to him. His smile twitched a bit bigger, then relaxed. "Nope, it's not too bad at all, as long as I don't have to look at those fish." I opened the ice chest.

The cans of beer were nearly gone. Two fish that had died rested in the ice. I pushed them aside. Through the ice I could see three cans decorated red, white, and blue. They looked like wet pieces of a jittery jigsaw puzzle.

"There's no soda," I said, after pawing through the cold wetness. Uncle Wing did not move. Hadn't he been responsible for getting drinks for everyone? I couldn't remember. "There's nothing in here for me to drink," I said to him.

Suddenly my mouth and throat were so dry I could barely stand it. What was left of the corn bread was grainy on my tongue.

"I sure am thirsty," I said loudly. If Papa and Uncle Wing woke up, one of them could run me to a 7-Eleven. I could get one of those humongous drinks, the kind big enough for a small army. But neither of them moved. I thought I heard my throat creak when I swallowed.

A huge, slow fly buzzed near the picnic basket. I flipped the lid shut with a *pop!*

"How could they have forgotten me?" I said to the fly. It walked along the top of the basket, then stopped and washed its face. I looked over at the fish. "Boy, am I ever thirsty." One white belly flashed at me. I wondered if any more of them were dead. Was my flounder?

The February sun beat down on me like an August one. I scooped my hand into the river and slurped the saltiness down. The salt dried my tongue instantly. Now I was so thirsty I thought I would die for sure.

Then I had it. I knew I shouldn't do it. I knew better because Momma and Daddy had taught me all my life I shouldn't. There could be bad problems when kids my age did what I was about to do. But right then, at that very thirsty moment, there didn't seem any other way.

"I'm drinking me a beer," I said. Uncle Wing

didn't say a word. Papa kept ahold of his own drink. Up and down, up and down it went with his breathing.

"Yes sirree, that's what I'm gonna do," I said, giving them a chance to wake up. Neither moved. I dug into the ice chest and pulled open a red, white, and blue can. "If I don't drink this," I said to the fly and the fish and the egret that had flown away, "if I don't drink this, I know I'm gonna die from thirst. And there's already been too much dying going on. I just can't stand it anymore." I popped the top on the beer and held my nose with my other hand. Then I drank down a quarter of it.

The beer was so cold and so wet that at first I thought it actually tasted good. When I let loose of my nose, though, I realized it might have been better just to die. I remember hearing someone say that he would rather puke than drink a beer. Momma is always saying that desperate people will do desperate things. Now I knew what both Momma and that man meant.

My tongue was still as stiff as a board, so I held my nose again and drank some more. I belched a huge burp that tasted just as bad as the beer had. Thankfully, though, my thirst was gone. I'd be okay now.

As soon as I thought it, my thirst was raging again. The sun was pounding down hotter and hotter. I knew it wasn't noon yet, but what would happen when it was? I'd be so thirsty then, I'd probably be unable to move.

"I better just finish off this can of beer," I said, looking over the edge of the boat again, to where the fish were. "I know I shouldn't, but I should. Shouldn't, should." I snickered. There was a long, beautiful egret feather floating next to the boat. I reached down and got it. Droplets of water dripped off the snowy white feather.

"Wow," I said softly. I'd never been this close to an egret before. No, wait a minute, that didn't make sense. The only time I ever saw egrets were in books or from a long way off. Now I was practically holding one in my hand. I knew what I meant even if I couldn't think it right.

I stuck the feather behind my ear. It crossed my mind there might be bugs on it, but then I decided no, egrets were just too pretty to have bugs.

My first beer was gone now. So I opened a second. I rolled the cold can between my hands. The cool wetness of the metal seemed to soothe away a sadness that had been sitting in my heart all morning. Perhaps I was rolling off my fingerprints too. Well, it didn't matter. I wasn't thirsty anymore.

"This beer's not so bad except for the taste," I said to the can on Papa's stomach. It rose up, up, up with one breath and came down ever so slowly. "I love fishing too. And birds. And flies." I raised my drink to the fly that walked carefully around the lip of Papa's beer. I would have to remember to tell him to wipe that off before taking another drink. A shiver went over me as I thought of all the germs that were being tracked by the fly. Other than the germs, though, I knew that it was a very nice fly and that no real harm was intended.

When the last can of beer was gone, and all the grapes and the three candy bars Momma had packed as a treat, I gently removed the can from Papa's fingers. I wiped the top and then the sides and finally the bottom of the can carefully with my shirttail. Then I drank it too. It was warm and sad-tasting. No, I was sad.

"It's these poor fish," I said to the drink. "These poor, poor fish. And all the egrets."

I thought of Kelly and how sad she would be about the worms and fish and egrets and fat, slow flies. I thought about how sad she would be about my fingerprints being gone, and all the germs the fly was spreading, and the fact that Papa's hair would never be blond again and that probably Uncle Wing would not try to patent his incredible bait intensi-fier. I thought of her being dead and my being alive. It just wasn't right. I was the one who always thought up crazy things to do. She always did every-thing she was asked, most often the very first time. Guilt crept up into my throat. "Kelly," I said.

Something had to be done. I had to do something because Kelly was not here to do it. But what? I held the red, white, and blue can in my hand, and I suddenly felt very American. I would never litter again. If I only could remember the tune of a patriotic song, darn it, I would hum it. I looked over the side of the boat.

My head swam beside the fish as I pulled the line up and out of the water. I unsnapped the giant hook and pulled the fish off one at a time. My flounder was first.

I kissed it on the open mouth, then set it gently on the surface of the water. It sat there a second, smiling at me. I smiled back.

"Don't die," I said, wiping tears from my cheeks. "Dive. Dive," I said, quoting a line from one of my favorite movies. Which one it was I couldn't quite remember, except that it was a very funny line. I laughed. The fish slipped from my sight with a silver flash, and it was gone.

I kissed each fish good-bye. It was a celebration. An American celebration of freedom. This was a celebration fighting death. Why hadn't I thought of this for Kelly? If I had, maybe she would be here now. If I had thought of this for Kelly, maybe I could have saved her.

I was wearing an extremely large egret feather behind my ear. It was so large and heavy that my head cocked to that side. Soon my head would be lying flat on my shoulder. But that was okay, because I was an American who would never litter again.

Just as I was kissing the last bass good-bye, Uncle Wing stood huge in the boat.

"What in the hell are you doing, Leah?" he shouted.

Papa sat up with a jerk.

"Fighting the battle of independence for the fish." I knew there was a song I could sing right then that would go perfectly with all this, but I could only remember the words.

"When Johnny comes marching home again," I said softlike to Papa and Uncle Wing. I wanted them to understand how important it was to sing along. I wanted to shout, "Join in everybody. Sing. Sing as loud as you can," but my stomach was really hurting.

"Ask the fly, Uncle Wing," I said. Then I threw up in the water.

The whole ride home I felt like I was riding tidal wave after tidal wave of grief. I was so upset about Kelly, sure I could have done something to save her, like I had saved the fish.

I cried all the way home and talked all the way to Papa about dying and how it wasn't fair. Not to anyone or anything. Not the worms or the fish or the egrets nearly extinct. Or to Kelly. I told him and Uncle Wing that God hadn't thought things out, that I should have been the one to die, that Kelly was the good one. I tried to explain to them that good people shouldn't die. Papa just smoothed my hair and said things I couldn't remember later.

Uncle Wing carried me into the house. Papa explained everything to Momma. She tucked me into bed after a bath.

Nobody was mad at me. Not even Uncle Wing. He said we had proved the secret bait intensifier worked. Everyone was real quiet so I could sleep. I didn't think I'd be able to. But when I woke up, it was very late. My stomach was growling from being so empty, and I was surprised that I didn't have a pounding headache, just a slight throb.

I decided to get up. I padded lightly down the stairs to the kitchen. I opened the fridge and dug through it, trying to find something to eat. I avoided the cold chicken and grapes. I settled on a salad.

I left the lights out and went into the dining room. Moonlight streamed in through the lacy curtains. I sat down and started to eat.

In the dining room, where Kelly had fallen to the floor so long ago, I realized that there wasn't anything I could have done to save her. Kelly was gone, and I couldn't have stopped her from going. Because. Because? That answer I didn't know. I could only hold her hand while she was dying. I could

only whisper to her that I loved her and scream for
Momma and then the ambulance men to help her.
That was all I could do. It made my throat tight to
think it.

I rinsed my salad bowl in the sink. The water
splashed up on the backboard. I took a striped dish-
cloth and wiped it dry. In the moonlight my hands
looked like the bellies of the fish under the water.
Pale. My nails were bitten low. I needed to stop that
habit.

In slow motion I started up the stairs to my room.
I let my hand drag up the oak rail. It was satiny
smooth. I walked past Momma and Daddy's room.

"Are you okay?" Momma said, soft like the moon
coming in through their window. She followed me
into my room.

"Yes," I lied.

"Papa told me something you said today," she
said, sitting on the edge of my bed. I pulled the covers up to my chin and waited.

"He said that you thought that maybe you should
have been the one to die. And not Kelly."

There was a cold feeling inside me.

"Nobody should ever die," I said. "But especially
not good people. They should keep on going forever."

"People's bodies get tired of living," Momma
said. "Or there's something wrong in them that
makes them quit working."

I lay quiet for a moment.

"I keep thinking that maybe it should have been me," I said at last. "She was so good."

"Leah," Momma said. She sounded shocked. "Daddy and I wanted you both. Always. Neither one of us could choose which of our children should live or die. I want both of my girls. I loved Kelly and you the same. With all my heart."

"But she was so good."

"You aren't bad."

"I know. It's just . . . she did the things you asked. You never had to ask her twice. Somebody that good is easier to love than somebody like me."

Momma sighed real deep.

"When I married your daddy, I thought I would never be able to love anyone as much as I did him. A couple of years later you came along, and I was surprised to find that I had more love inside me. I wasn't trying to split it in half. It had doubled. When Kelly came along a year later, there was even more than before. It never got less. It never will. It just keeps on growing."

Momma sat with me awhile longer. She talked to me low until my eyelids were so heavy I couldn't open them again. Then she got up catlike and padded from the room. There was a softness inside me now, soft like the smell of the soap Momma washes with, that told me Kelly was wanted at home. And so was I.

March

BIKING HOME

Knowing Momma and Daddy weren't sorry I was alive made me feel lighter. It eased my guilt that I was living and Kelly was dead. That doesn't mean I completely forgot about Kelly. In fact, for some reason, in the beginning, school seemed the hardest to bear. I don't know why.

At home there were all kinds of reminders of Kelly. But there were all kinds of comforts too. If I went into our room—my room—there was everything that Kelly had had. We hadn't changed any of it. Kelly's bed was still opposite mine. There was a big poster of a bunch of wild horses running fierce across the plains, above her headboard. Her little pink alarm clock was on her dresser, and all her clothes were in the drawers. On her half of the bedside table was a cup with arms stretched all the way around it. It said, "I love you this much."

Even Kelly's shoes were lined up neatly in our walk-in closet. Her book bag was on the corner of the dresser, full of new school supplies, waiting, because Kelly had died the first morning of school. I guess I was waiting too. Anyway, Momma and Daddy had talked about moving Kelly's things out, but neither had made a move to do it. I was secretly glad.

Sometimes, if I was really sad and hurting, I'd go in the bedroom and lie on Kelly's bed. It smelled like her still. I'd sniff real deep, burying my face into her pillow, then close my eyes and remember her. Remember us. And sometimes I'd feel better.

Or I'd go into the closet and touch her clothes. Touch the things that had been her favorites, like her blue denim dress, sewn with pink thread around all the seams and pockets. It seemed strange to me that I'd keep on growing and changing, and so would the things on my side of the closet. But never Kelly's. Not ever her things. They would always be the same.

Even though there was pain in every corner of my house, there was also someone standing close by to help wade through the feelings that were pulling me down. And sometimes, I think, I helped Momma or Daddy or Papa too.

But school . . . school was different.

I knew it would be that way too. That's why I didn't even start back until a few days into December. I probably wouldn't have even gone then, but I knew with Christmas coming up, I was going to need some kind of distraction. School was it. Daddy had worried that I would fall behind, but Momma sided with me, telling him no one could learn anything with all the stress we were going through. I guess because Daddy went right back to work, he thought I could handle school. But never once did he push me.

My school was a small enough place that almost everyone knew Kelly was dead. Some of the teachers and even the principal came to her funeral. But knowing something doesn't necessarily mean you know what to do about that situation. And so no one knew how to treat me.

Even Tom, my very best friend outside my family, didn't know what to do when he was around me for the first little while after Kelly's death. It was really awkward.

I was back to school one week and he wouldn't even talk to me. Anytime he'd see me, he'd turn and go the other way. Then one day he ran up to me on the playground to where I was sitting alone on the merry-go-round. He hugged my head real tight because I was sitting and he was standing. Then he started crying and ran off home. He didn't come back to school that day or even the next. But after that things were better between us.

So except for Tom, I was pretty much alone at school. And when the memories would come, there was just no getting by them. There was no one to hold me up.

I remember this one time when I was about eight years old. Momma and Daddy and Kelly and I were on our way to the Wednesday night meeting at the big Baptist church. We were going for Bible study and then to choir practice, except for Daddy, who doesn't really do much of any kind of singing except maybe to hum real soft.

Anyway, we had just pulled into the parking lot and were getting out of the car when the side doors of the church burst open and Annie Neilson came staggering out, crying and screaming. Annie Nielson was a member of our congregation even though her husband, Kevin, refused to join. It seemed like the preacher was always praying to have Kevin's heart softened so that Annie wouldn't have to sit alone in church anymore. Not that she did sit alone, but you know what I mean.

Grammy was with her, and three other ladies, and they were dragging her out of the building, holding her up, practically carrying her. Daddy ran over there, thinking that maybe Annie was sick and he could carry her to her car. He came back after a second, looking real upset.

"Annie's husband was killed in a car accident on his way to do some night shrimping," he said, and that was all. We didn't even go in to sing. We just turned around and went back home. And I kept thinking about how Annie couldn't stand alone and how sad she was.

Now, sometimes, I feel how Annie looked. Only there are no old ladies to drag me where I need to go.

At the very end of March two things happened: The weather turned so cold that it snowed some places in Florida. And a girl moved into the seventh grade. Her name was Vickie Abernathy, and she and her mother and little sister came down from North Florida so her mom could start teaching at the local community college.

Sometimes being new in a school or a town can be hard. And getting to know people can be tough. If things had been different in my life, Kelly and I would have probably made good friends with Vickie.

I mean, she looked okay. She had real curly brownish blond hair and lots of freckles and huge brown eyes. Her nose was crooked, and she was pretty short compared to me. I made up my mind right in the middle of science, when Vickie came in and introduced herself to the class, that I didn't need anyone to be my friend right now. I could see that she had been crying, and I felt a little sorry for her. Before, I might have thought any seventh grader crying was just a big baby. Now, I was struggling hard enough just trying to get up the energy to do my homework.

Two days after she started school, Vickie came up to me. I was sitting in the back of the room with Tom, working out some math problems.

"Hi!" she said to us, and she smiled big. "Hi, Leah." She sat down at the round table, right next to me, and pulled out her math worksheet. "I've already done this stuff in Gainesville. It's pretty easy. Do y'all need any help?" Her accent was thick, and southern, like Papa's.

I shook my head, and so did Tom. I looked back down at my paper. Maybe I did need some help. Math wasn't seeming too important to me. Or English. Or anything, for that matter. I guess I really needed help in thinking that school was important to me.

The three of us sat quietly working out problems. When we were finished, Tom gathered up our papers and carried them up to Mrs. Dinkins.

While he was gone, Vickie leaned close to me. I could feel her warm breath on my face.

"I heard about your sister," she said, "and I'm real sorry. It doesn't seem right, does it?"

I looked into her eyes. She was getting ready to cry, and I realized that I was too. That wasn't unusual for me. But this stranger, this new girl in my class? She hadn't even known Kelly and here she was crying.

I shook my head no. No, it didn't seem right. Nothing seemed right to me. Not Kelly. Not math. Not even Vickie.

"I've thought a lot about death, and it's a hard one to figure out. I just can't understand it." She shrugged her shoulders, then breathed real deep.

She smelled like peppermints. "You want to be best friends?" she said.

Best friends? I thought. You don't ask to be best friends. It just happens. Tom was back. He leaned over the table where we were.

"Mrs. Dinkins wants us to go back to our seats now," he said. I was aware of the class coming to life. The sound of papers being shuffled, book bag zippers closing, people whispering, and books being slammed shut. It must be nearly time to go home. I looked at the clock: two-twenty. Afternoon announcements would be coming on any minute and we'd be free. School days seemed to crawl by. I wanted to go home. Grandma and Uncle Wing were coming for their weekly Tuesday night visit.

I looked at Vickie. She was looking at me expectantly. I shook my head.

"No," I said. "I better not. Kelly was my best friend. Thanks, though."

A bell was ringing in the back of my head. I realized it was the dismissal bell. I stood there, though, with my mouth hanging open. Tom pulled on me.

"Let's go," he said. "I'll ride home with you."

I kept standing there and so did Vickie.

"Maybe you could come to my house and spend the night or something," she said. Vickie turned and left the classroom. In a minute I could see her from the window, walking out to the buses.

"Let's go home," said Tom. "It's starting to cloud up. I think it's going to rain again."

"I don't want to go home right away," I said. "Maybe you should go on without me." My legs were feeling all rubbery.

"Naw," said Tom. "Unless you don't want me to go with you. I like riding bikes in the cold. Maybe it'll snow on us." That's what Tom and I had been praying for. One inch of snow and the school would be shut down forever. Or at least a day.

I laughed, and Tom grinned at me. Good old Tom.

Isn't it funny how you don't see people, how they look, after a while? You only see them as they truly are. Take, for example, Tom. I had to look real hard to see his outside, because I'm so used to the way he acts, the way he really is.

See, Tom has always been Tom to me. We've been friends forever. And he's always been nice. He's never been like the other guys who punch you or say mean things when you walk past in the lunchroom.

There were girls in my grade who said Tom was the cutest boy in all of New Smyrna Middle School. Looking at him now, I could see maybe that he was. His hair is light brown and his eyes are dark blue. He has maybe five freckles that dot his nose. When he smiles his eyes get real squinty so that it looks like he can't even see. His teeth are really white and straight, but that's because his uncle is an orthodontist in Daytona.

Tom's face was starting to turn a little pink because I was looking at him so hard. My stomach did a funny flip-flop. Suddenly I was embarrassed too, so I crossed my eyes at him. We went to get our coats and backpacks, then outside to get our bikes.

The weather was pretty cold, and the sky was getting black. I could smell the ocean. Every once in a while there'd be a puff of warm air, but while we were standing by the bicycle rack unlocking our bikes, the last warm puff swooshed in and then out.

Winter was definitely visiting Florida. Tonight people would be lighting the smudge pots in the orange groves to keep the fruit from freezing.

Tom lives only a couple of blocks from me. Just two houses catty-corner from where Grandma and Uncle Wing bought their house. We decided that it would be a good idea to bicycle near where we lived. We could go the long way home and, if there was time, maybe ride through the old Sugar Mill.

As soon as we started off toward home, I realized that we had made a mistake by choosing the long way. For one thing the first mile or two we couldn't ride side by side because of afternoon traffic. And then, five minutes after we left the school grounds, the wind off the ocean started blowing in so strong that I could almost taste the salt. It was so cold my fingers were turning blue. Why hadn't I brought gloves? The next thing I knew my nose was running like a faucet. Normally I wouldn't have cared that

much about a runny nose, I would have just sniffed
a lot and wiped my sleeve across my face, but now
that I noticed how cute Tom was, I didn't want him
to hear me snorting like a pig. It wasn't that things
had changed between us. It was just . . . well, I
don't know.

I pedaled as close to Tom's back tire as I dared,
hoping that he would shield me from the wind.
Mostly, though, his tire just spit pebbles at me. Tears
were being torn out of my eyes. I wondered if it was
cold enough to freeze them. That might be funny.

But after a little more pedaling, nothing was
funny. And it became even worse when the clouds
cracked open and dumped enough water on Tom
and me to fill a river.

Every once in a while Tom would look back and
holler at me to see if I was okay. He caught me
wiping my nose on my sleeve only twice. The rain
hit us, stinging like tiny rocks. Then it became hail
and it felt more like bits of glass. But things could
have been worse. The hail could have been the golf-
ball size which I have seen fall from the skies on
more than one occasion.

We splashed through puddles that covered entire
sections of the road. We pedaled squiggly lines
through mud. The trees looked dark green, wet, and
drippy. I think the sun had taken a break. It looked
like dusk out, but it couldn't have been any more
than three-thirty in the afternoon. When I could, I

pedaled up next to Tom. Now I didn't care if my nose fell off my face and landed right in front of him. I just wanted to get home and change out of these clothes. We were pumping furiously.

"Hey!" Tom said. I looked over at him. His nose was as red as mine felt. I couldn't help grinning. If both of our noses were red, that was okay. A car passed us and beeped long at me. I was out too far in the road. As it passed, it splashed a spray of water that rolled toward us like a wave. I jerked my bike toward safety and smacked right into Tom. Both of us wobbled and swerved, and then finally we crashed, skidding into the deep ditch that ran alongside the road. Icy water rushed over me. Long ditch weeds bowed with the wind, whipping down toward us, then straightened as the wind sucked in its breath to let out another tremendous blow.

I was tangled with my bike and Tom and his bike. My wrist hurt, and there was mud and grass on my face. My nose and ears were throbbing with the cold. The hail was getting bigger, splashing in the water around us.

"Hey," Tom said. "You wanna go on up to the Sugar Mill?"

I just laughed. Good old Tom.

April

THE ACCIDENT

Not all of Uncle Wing's inventions were a success.

There was one time, before he and Grandma moved to New Smyrna to be closer to my daddy, that Uncle Wing tried to make a golf ball that packed so much power that only a tiny tap from a club would send it flying. He spent many an hour on the golf course thinking and experimenting. At least that's what he told Grandma. Grandma said that wasn't true. She said he was just taking it easy in the Florida sun. His invention was proof, she said.

When Uncle Wing finally came up with some ideas, he locked himself in the basement of their old house. This is what Uncle Wing always does when he's in the developmental stage of a project: he puts himself in a place where no one can bother him or tempt him away from what he is doing. He came out only to eat and go to the bathroom and to sleep. After four days he emerged from the basement with the golf ball. Actually, Grandma said it looked something like a golf ball. It was about the size of one, but it didn't have a white dimpled cover on it.

Uncle Wing came into the kitchen with the ball sitting like a brown egg in the palm of his hand.

"This is it, Mom," he said to Grandma, and then he went to shower so he'd be good and clean when they tested it. Grandma used to go to all the first testings of any of Uncle Wing's inventions. For luck.

To make a long story short, when Uncle Wing teed up and hit that ball, there was an explosion that was heard a mile away and golf ball debris shot forty feet in every direction. One piece hit Grandma so hard in the glasses that it knocked her flat on her bottom. There was even a small cut on the bridge of her nose. And for nearly a month Uncle Wing was saying "Excuse me?" to everything that anyone would say to him because he was having a hard time hearing.

"At least he had manners," Grandma said, each time she finished telling the golf-ball story. Then everybody would laugh or say just how fortunate she was to have had her glasses on that day and not her contact lenses. Grandma got to thinking about that and decided from that golf ball–exploding day and on she would wait until Uncle Wing's ideas were proved on somebody else. She didn't want to risk a glass eye.

"Aaaw, come on, Mom," said Uncle Wing when she would conclude the story, announcing that she no longer attended the unveiling ceremonies because she did not want a glass eye. "I could invent one for you." This always got a big laugh too, but both Grandma and Uncle Wing were serious.

Uncle Wing put the golf ball idea on a back burner to simmer for a while. One Saturday morning Papa announced that there was to be a great invention unveiling at Uncle Wing's house and that Momma, Daddy, Papa, and I were invited. I wondered if it was the golf ball and if I should wear safety glasses.

"Bowing out graciously, are you?" said Papa when Daddy told him they were going out to look for a new car. "Well, you two do need a new car." I wholeheartedly agreed. We'd had that old Chevy forever and a day.

"Don't blame us if Wing only includes us in on the fame. Not that we won't deserve it," Papa said, grinning big at me. "Let's us head on over," he said, and we started the two-block walk over. The blocks in our neighborhood are real big because everybody has at least a third of an acre.

"Papa," I said, "I sure wish Kelly were going with us."

"Me, too, honey." Papa slipped his hand into mine. The sun beat down warm on our heads. The heat danced in waves above the blacktop road, shimmering and like silver. In the ditch next to the road where we walked, water trickled through thick green grass. I closed Mrs. Comer's mailbox when we passed it. On one side it said " omer." I thought about getting a stick-on *C* later on. We passed Ricky and Ryan, the twins. They were fighting in the front yard. Their little sister was swinging back and forth in a windup swing. I waved to Linda Diamond, a girl in my class, who was standing on her side lawn, watering huge pink hydrangea flowers.

Papa and I walked along the road till we came to an empty lot. Here the weeds were tall and wildflowers grew thick and beautiful. Papa stepped on the barbed wire, opening a hole for me to climb through the fence that surrounded the lot. Then he climbed through too. We began to push our way through the growth. The flowers nodded at us with the breeze. Every once in a while a bigger gust of wind would push through the field, and like a wave, the flowers and grasses would lean closer to the ground.

In the distance I could see dark clouds appearing. A summer storm was on its way. My hair moved around my face.

"I dreamed Kelly wasn't dead," I said. Grasshoppers were jumping up from in front of us, hopping this way and that. "She didn't know she was dead either, and she was crying. I woke up hoping, but her bed was still empty." I breathed deep as a warm wind rushed at me, bringing with it the smells of hot grass. The frogs were begging for rain. Another breeze blew, and a lump came up in my throat. I didn't tell him I woke up crying and calling her name.

"I still dream about your grandmother," Papa said. "Nowhere as often as I used to."

"How can you stand it, Papa?"

"It isn't as painful as it was. I've had years to heal."

"But I don't think I could stand years of this," I said. A puff of cool wind smoothed against my face. The weather sure was acting strange this year. By April things should be warming up good, not so much cold. Maybe we were paying for the fishing in February now.

"It gets easier to bear," Papa said.

"Sometimes I feel like I can't breathe."

Papa nodded and was quiet. "It gets easier, but you never forget the person you loved. They're always warm in your memories."

"But for how much longer?" I said. I could see Uncle Wing waiting in his front yard.

"I couldn't tell you, Leah. It's different for everybody, but I promise it won't last forever."

Uncle Wing looked up. "Hurry," he shouted when he saw Papa and me on the road. He was waving his arms at us. "There's a storm coming. We've got to hurry."

We were walking fast now. The wind nudged us from behind.

"Hey, Wing," Papa said, "is everything set?"

Uncle Wing walked out to the road to meet us. He rubbed his hands together like he was cold. His clean face was shining with excitement.

"Papa," Uncle Wing said, "this is it. This is probably going to be the invention that I am remembered the most for. Follow me."

"Don't forget to include Leah and me if there are any pictures taken," Papa said.

Papa and I followed Uncle Wing into the backyard where an old Toyota truck was parked.

"Let me explain what I have created," Uncle Wing said. His face was shiny. His hair was still wet from showering. A breeze blew from the north and then from the east. The smell of the ocean was strong.

"It occurred to me, whilst driving my old truck"—Uncle Wing waved in the direction of his pickup and boat, parked under an old shade tree—"that I could very possibly make a car that could be driven completely by buttons."

He led us to the old powder blue truck. It had definitely seen better days. In fact, it looked just about as bad as Uncle Wing's old rattletrap, except, of course, it didn't have a boat permanently attached.

Opening the driver's door, Uncle Wing nodded that we should take a peek into the cab. The upholstery was so torn up that hard, crusty yellow foam poked out everywhere. In four or five places I could even see rust-colored springs.

The wind whistled around Grandma's house, tugging at my hair. Papa's shirttails snapped and slapped like tiny flags.

"Ooo-eee," said Papa. "Would you look at that! Wing, that dash looks like the control panel of a small plane."

Uncle Wing bowed his head in modesty. The wind pushed me against the car, then pulled me away. The air gleamed yellow.

I looked back into the truck. Yep, sure enough, there was a new dashboard. And talk about buttons and switches. This was definitely something new.

"I figured it this way," said Uncle Wing. "Why not be able to drive in complete and utter comfort? Driving should be a joy."

I looked back into the truck again, my eyebrows raised. There was no way that sitting on that old seat was going to make anyone feel any joy. It would probably even be painful.

Papa was nodding his head up and down. The wind was getting stronger and stronger. Then suddenly it stopped, and the air hung heavy and damp.

Uncle Wing climbed into the cab. He slammed the door shut after two tries. Then he started to unroll the window. It would go down only three inches.

He lifted his lips toward the crack and hollered to us. "Now stand way back from me until I get this thing agoing."

I ran up onto the tiny side porch, where Grandma had set two large cement flower pots full of red geraniums. The air on the porch was thick with the bitter smell of the flowers. I could hear the television playing one of Grandma's favorite soap operas. Her eyes would definitely be safe in there.

After a few tries Uncle Wing got the engine to start.

"Just the push of a button," said Uncle Wing, pointing a finger out the window. Only he had to yell it at us because there was no muffler on the truck.

Papa whooped and loped to the side of the cab. Uncle Wing grinned at Papa.

I stepped a few feet off the porch. That's when I noticed that the sky had taken on a greenish gray tint.

"Oh, my gosh," I said.

A small gray funnel cloud was slowly dancing its way toward Grandma's yard.

"Tornado," I screeched.

"Just like a tornado," Papa said, smiling big at me.

Uncle Wing gave me a thumbs-up sign. He was gunning the motor. For one second I wondered if he was using his finger on a button or the gas pedal.

There was a rumbling noise that sounded like a train, and I could feel the ground shaking a bit, but Papa and Uncle Wing never even noticed. The truck was just too loud.

I started to run out to Papa. Then I saw Uncle Wing lean sideways in the cab. He stretched his long legs out and rested them on the dash. I ran back toward the porch.

"Grandma," I screamed. "Grandma."

She came to the door quickly. "Tornado warnings on TV," she said.

"It's here," I yelled, only I was sure she couldn't hear me. I pointed to her backyard.

Suddenly the truck backfired, and without a warning it leaped into reverse. Papa didn't even have a chance to run. The back of the truck hit him hard and knocked him down, running over both his legs.

Uncle Wing switched the engine off before the front tires ran over Papa too. He shoved hard against the cab door, to get out. But he was stuck. The air was a frenzy now. I thought I might be deaf from the sound of the tornado. Nobody but me and Grandma even knew that it was in the yard.

Papa was rolling a little, from side to side, in between the front tires and the back ones.

"Papa," said Uncle Wing; only I couldn't hear him, I just read his lips. His face was all red and scared. He was yelling out the three-inch crack in the window. "Papa." I saw him drop his head into his hands.

The tornado roared into the side yard, whipping and tearing at my clothes, pulling my hair. I grabbed hold of Grandma and then held on to the porch railing. A bad taste came into my mouth. I wanted to run, but my legs felt like pieces of ice. I couldn't move them.

Grandma screamed and so did I, but it was as if neither one of us had made a sound. I had never been this close to a tornado before. It pushed and pulled me. The geraniums bent low in the pots. Paper whisked around the yard. The air seemed to vibrate. Rain and hail spattered on the ground. It was one of the scariest things I have ever seen in my life.

The tornado slid over toward Uncle Wing and Papa and the powder blue Toyota truck, and there was nothing that we could do. Sand stung my face and hands.

The tornado jumped into the bed of the truck and lifted it gently into the air, spinning it once, then a second time. It carried the Toyota to the ditch and set it gently down. Papa was lying openmouthed on his side, finally seeing one of nature's wildest wonders leap out of the yard and toward the road.

Uncle Wing was staring wide-eyed from the cab. The whole thing reminded me of a slow-motion movie.

Grandma was clutching her bosom with one hand. The other was covering her nose and mouth. My knuckles were white where I was holding on to her wrist.

"Papa," I said, and ran out to where he was lying. "Papa."

"I will be cat-kicked," said Papa, in a real weak voice.

Uncle Wing came running over to where we were. He had rolled down the window on the passenger's side of the truck and squeezed through it. He was running crooked and tears were streaming down his face.

"What have I done? What have I done?" he kept saying over and over again.

"You run over me, Wing," said Papa. He started to laugh, then stopped. "Maybe I should go into the house. I'm not feeling too good. Help me up, Wing."

"Don't you dare move," said Grandma. "We have to call Nine-one-one." Her hands were shaking so badly I could hardly believe it. I couldn't believe anything that had just happened. But Papa was on the ground and the truck was in the ditch and there was garbage and stuff strewn all over the yard from the tornado.

"Hell," said Papa in a funny voice, "I'm not lying here forever. There's a tornado on the loose. Didn't you just see that?"

"Grandma's right, Papa," I said. "Somebody run over by a truck should never stand up. I saw it on a television program that you should never move an injured victim unless there is a worse danger nearby."

"Leah," Papa said, almost shouting, "that was a tornado. It is a worse danger. I want to get into the house where I can hide under a bed if it comes back."

"I don't think it's coming back," I said. But Uncle Wing was already pulling Papa to his feet.

One of Papa's leg snapped, and he fell back to the ground with a yell.

Uncle Wing stood, swallowed, and said, "Mom, call an ambulance." Then he fainted and fell flat on his face. I nearly threw up when I heard his nose hit the ground.

"Well, I will be cat-kicked," Papa said again. Only real soft this time. Then he closed his eyes and waited for the ambulance to arrive.

NEW SMYRNA—Irwing Johnson Orton had the ride of his life on Tuesday afternoon, when a tornado lifted his small pickup truck and set it down in a ditch. Orton was at the wheel of his vehicle when the event occurred.

Although Orton was uninjured by the tornado, he did break his nose in a fall related to a car accident involving an elderly relative.

Orton was released from Fish Memorial Hospital after treatment for shock and a broken nose.

Irwing Orton is well known for his many inventions and was working perfecting his latest when the recent tornado struck at his residence at 850 West Palmetto Drive.

NEW SMYRNA BEACH VFW NEWS—Morgan "Papa" Sinclair is resting quietly in room 604 of Fish Memorial Hospital.

Papa was run over by Irwing Orton on Tuesday afternoon, prior to the tornado that touched down that same day. His left leg is broken.

Papa says he welcomes all visitors.

Well, Papa got his wish to become famous with Uncle Wing because of an invention, but there were no pictures taken for the papers after all. Papa was a little disappointed.

May

TOM AND ME

School was out the end of May. I think every kid in New Smyrna Middle School was excited about it except me. Normally I would have screamed as loud as the next person, running out of the building that last Friday. But the thought of a whole summer, a whole life of summers, without Kelly made me so sad that I went straight home, flopped myself on the bed, and started crying.

A whole summer. What in the world would I do? How could I make it even another minute alone?

It's interesting the way I was feeling. I'd be up one minute, or half a day, or maybe even two days in a row, feeling all right. I'd still miss Kelly and stuff, but it was like it was getting a little easier. I didn't expect her to be there around every turn anymore. It was like I was coming to accept her being gone. I didn't like it that she was gone, but it was easier to make it through a day.

Then, when I thought I'd be able maybe to stop missing her so much, something would remind me of her. Not just remind me of Kelly, but remind me of everything that had been about her. Her hair. The way she smelled. The way she laughed and cried and trusted people.

Since Kelly's death I had aged one thousand years in my guts. Maybe I looked the same on the outside, but on the inside, where all my feelings were, I had aged one thousand years. That old part of me would never change. I would never again be twelve years old. I was one thousand and twelve. And when September came again, I would be one thousand thirteen. And the following September I would be one thousand fourteen. Because September is when Kelly had died.

I talked with Tom about the way I was feeling. It was the last day in May, a week since school had gotten out, and he decided that it was high time to get me out of the house, where I'd been mooning around.

"We're getting out of here," he said. Tom practically pulled me out of the house.

Both of our bicycles were parked in the front yard.

I didn't realize how much I had missed the sun and the warm air. I had missed the smells and sounds of being outside. I had missed Tom too. As soon as I stepped off the porch, it felt like a big shadow lifted from my shoulders.

We got on our bicycles and started pedaling. Right down Adeline Street, back down the woodsy part of the neighborhood, toward the old Sugar

Mill. Already it was summerlike, and not even ten in the morning. The sun was white-hot, frying down on us. I rode beside Tom. The wind blew and tugged at our hair. The sun made our eyes squint. I loved it.

Without speaking, we turned into the mill. We rode along the dirt path, past a sign that said WELCOME TO THE OLD SUGAR MILL USED SINCE THE 1800S. No one is really sure just how long the mill has been in existence. But it's been preserved for a good long time. Papa even remembers visiting here when he was a little boy.

Huge oak and pine trees covered the area. Palmetto trees with limbs like ladder rungs dotted here and there. Scrub brush edged the entire mill, like a planned hedge. There was a large grassy place and then the old mill.

I guess that the mill isn't that fantastic, except for the fact that it is so old.

A small river runs through the property, right next to a small coquina rock building, where the boiling of the cane sugar took place. Outside was the mill itself. This is where the sugarcane was ground, squeezing out the sweet juices to be made into syrup or sugar.

We pedaled past all this, back to where there was a paved footpath.

Now this is one of the strange things about the old mill. Some family that owned all this land, before giving it to New Smyrna city, had six huge concrete dinosaurs built. This happened way back in the olden days, but not so long ago that they were here for Papa to see. Lots of the information about the way dinosaurs looked and lived have changed. There used to be signs that told about these creatures, but some schoolteachers from the old high school, which has since been rebuilt, had those taken down and destroyed because they had so much wrong information. These same teachers wanted the dinosaurs destroyed, but some people who were kids when the dinosaurs were built protested, and so they're still here.

Tom and I parked our bicycles and climbed up onto something that looked like a triceratops. It's probably fifteen feet long and painted purple. There are chips and gouges knocked out of it.

Tom was steering, and I was riding the long tail. Mockingbirds sang in the trees. Robins and cardinals and bluebirds flew around, sometimes fighting, sometimes preening. Bugs buzzed. Butterflies flew jagged paths through the air. The leaves rustled from a slight breeze. The grass was thick and green and particularly tall around the dinosaur toenails.

"Hey," Tom said, after a while, "I got an air rifle for Christmas from my uncle the orthodontist."

"Yeah?" I said. "Have you gone shooting with it?"

"Naw," Tom said. "Not that much. My uncle wants me to go hunting with him in the fall. He has all those girls in his family and no boys, so he kinda uses me to be his son." Tom was lying on his back, the middle horn of the triceratops supporting him; his legs were thrown over the shield.

"I don't shoot guns," I said. "Not anymore."

Tom started laughing, and then I joined him. Momma and Daddy still complained about having to have Elmo with the One Elbow, one of Papa's friends, come fix the ceiling after I accidentally shot six bullets through the mattress of their king-size bed and into the ceiling one night when I thought there was a werewolf in the house.

"I bet," Tom said. He sat real quiet. Then he got serious. "The thing is this: My uncle wants me to go hunting, and I don't wanna. I don't wanna kill anything."

"Yeah?" I said. I could understand not wanting to kill anything especially now that Kelly was gone. But I thought that all guys wanted to shoot stuff. You know, just to kill it.

"Yeah," Tom said, and he shook his head real sad-like.

I have to admit I was feeling pretty bad for Tom. Having friends can be hard work.

"Well," I said, "I'd be happy to help you out by giving you all the gun-shooting pointers that I know. But my daddy, he was real serious when he told me I was never to shoot his gun again. Course, not liking to shoot and not knowing how to shoot are two different things."

A bobwhite called its name soft and pretty and Tom whistled an answer. After a few minutes of calling back and forth with Tom, the brown bird poked its head out from bushes near an undersized *Tyrannosaurus rex*. Its head jerked this way and that as it checked for danger.

"I just can't see myself killing anything that beautiful," Tom said.

"Papa and Uncle Wing say those little ol' things are good eating," I said. But I had to agree with Tom. How could anyone kill anything on purpose?

"I just can't see killing anything myself," Tom said, and he shook his head back and forth like maybe killing was something that was supposed to be in a boy, and he had been born without that essential part.

"How about that old rooster at Mrs. Comer's?" I said, suddenly laughing. That bird was probably around in the days of the dinosaurs. He is so old and crazy that he's missing all his head feathers, and he crows all night long. It can get pretty annoying listening to him crow the sun's rising from 11:30 P.M. until the sun actually does come up.

Tom laughed too. "That old thing?" he said. "I'd probably be doing Mrs. Comer and all her chickens a favor to get rid of him."

"And anybody who walks onto her property," I said. This rooster also has a habit of chasing people out of Mrs. Comer's yard, and sometimes out of ours. He refuses to stay in the chicken yard that Daddy built for Mrs. Comer ages ago.

We sat quiet, just resting and thinking. It was an interesting feeling being with Tom. I peeked out at him every once in a while to see what he was doing. To see how he looked. Every time he looked at me, when I wasn't expecting it, my stomach flipped around. It was an exciting, unnerving feeling.

"Let's go get your gun and practice shooting tin cans at the dump," I said after a while. "That should be fun."

"I thought your daddy doesn't want you touching guns," Tom said.

I looked at him sideways. "He said I was never to touch his gun," I said. "And I won't ever do that again."

We ate lunch at Tom's house, then headed out with his air rifle slung over Tom's shoulder. I waved to Grandma when we went past her house. She was climbing into her car, probably going to volunteer at the library. She's always doing good deeds.

It took us only a little while to get to the dump.

Shooting there proved to be dang hot. We had just arrived, and already I could tell that I was getting one bad sunburn on my scalp where my hair was parted. I should have worn a baseball cap.

We stood out by a pile of old beat-up mattresses, pumped up the gun, and set up anything that was big as a trash can lid. We had already shot at pop cans and old beer bottles, but they were too small, and we kept missing.

"Get something bigger," Tom said after each miss.

I set up an old tire. Bang! We went over and checked out the tire. Not even a ding. "Can't believe I missed that too," he said.

"Probably because of that hole in the middle," I said.

"Probably," Tom said. "Get something bigger."

I finally found an old closet door. We dragged that from a pile of garbage and set it up the right way, tall. But Tom missed still. I was doing better than Tom, and this was only my second time with a real gun in my hand. After one of my shots and a thorough searching of the door we found a tiny knick on the very edge that I am sure had not been there before.

I finally came up with a winner of a plan. We set the door down longwise and then lay on our bellies to shoot. We also moved up until we were fifteen feet away. Boy, were we ever good at shooting now. We only missed a few times, but I'm sure that was because of the heat waves, rising shiny and shaky in between us and the target. Or because of the garbage itching at our bellies.

After a couple of hours shooting and using up the five whole boxes of Crossman pellets except for two that Tom wanted to be able to take home with him, we were experts. Now I bet we could have shot the eye out of a worm. Well, maybe a large, dead one. At close range.

At six o'clock we went home to my house for dinner. Tom hid the gun under the house with Daddy's tools and my fishing pole, so nobody would know what we had been doing, and we went in to eat.

After dinner I decided to ride home with Tom and visit with Grandma and Uncle Wing.

Right when we were getting onto our bikes, Mrs. Comer's rooster crowed at us from where he was hiding in the hibiscus hedge. He charged us, wings flapping furiously. He was kicking up pieces of grass, he was running so hard. His eyes were shining like two black glass beads.

"Watch out!" I said, and jumped on my bike. Tom followed me, his gun thumping on the seat of his bicycle, as he tried to run and jump on and ride and kick at the rooster at the same time. The rooster squawked happily at having chased us from my yard.

"I hate that ol' thing," I said.

Tom nodded in agreement.

We got almost to his house when Tom said, "Let's go back and scare that rooster."

"Sure," I said. "How are we gonna scare him? He'd flap us to death if we got too close to him."

Tom raised his eyebrows at me and grinned. "We're sharpshooters now, aren't we? We can sneak up behind him, and shoot right by his feet. We're dang good at shooting at the ground."

"Yeah," I said. "We are at that." I knew this to be a fact because we had been able to shoot so many pellets right into the ground, without even trying, both before we lay on our stomachs and then after.

"I bet if he saw it was you and me that shot at him, that rooster wouldn't bother you again." Tom was riding figure eights in the road, waiting for my decision. I had stopped and was standing on the yellow line that separated the two-lane road.

"All right," I said, a bit doubtfully. I really didn't think anything would ever scare that rooster. "But we have to be careful. If Momma or Daddy or Mrs. Comer sees us, we are in big trouble. You know I'm not supposed to shoot a gun."

"I thought you said you weren't supposed to shoot your daddy's gun?"

"And I never will." I held my fingers up the way Boy Scouts do.

"What d'you say?" Tom said.

"You lead," I said. "I'm following."

It was probably eight-thirty, and the sun was settling down to rest when we crept into Mrs. Comer's yard. We hid our bikes in the ditch down by Ricky and Ryan's, the twins', house. The rooster was sitting, bald and wiry, on the chicken yard fence.

"Uh-oh," I said. "You might not be able to scare

him, what with his sitting up there on the fence like that."

"Course I'll scare him," said Tom. "This is a gun, isn't it? And we're using almost real bullets, aren't we? You saw what we did to that door."

"Yeah," I said. "But the rooster didn't. Only a few seagulls were watching us."

Tom dropped the pellet into the gun and clicked it shut. The rooster looked directly at us when Tom started pumping up the gun.

Tom grinned at me. "He knows we're here," he said. "We will scare him after all."

"Better pump it up a few more times," I said. "So he really knows we mean business."

Tom rested the butt of the gun on his shoulder. "Maybe I oughta ask my uncle to get me a scope so I can get a little better at shooting cans and things," he said.

The rooster fluttered his wings and flew up into the warm breeze that pushed through the chicken yard to us, bringing with it the smell of chickens and warm manure. In slow motion he twisted in the air, then hit the ground and broke into a crow. He started to jog toward us.

"You better scare him quick," I said, backing up fast. "Or we're gonna be in a world of trouble."

"I'm aiming at his toes," said Tom, his jaw pressed tight to the smooth brown wood of the gun.

His speech was a little one-sided, and his lips looked all poky-outy. One eye was squinched halfway shut. Tom was backing up too.

Squh-wak, said the rooster. He was running faster now, kicking up dust and pebbles. Every once in a while he'd flap with his wings and push himself toward us with a great leap. There was a look of fire in his small black eyes.

"We better run for it," I said. "He's nearly fifteen feet away, and if he gets any closer, he's gonna be outa our practice range."

"I'm losing his feet in the sinking sun," said Tom. Then he pulled the trigger. "I've never shot while I was running before."

The rooster leaped high into the air, then ran in a crazy zigzag pattern, faster still.

"I think I scared him," said Tom, turning sideways and running. "No time for the second pellet." The gun was swinging and banging into his legs. I leaped backward over an Adirondack recliner that Mrs. Comer kept in the yard for when company came over. I bent down to hide behind it. There was no way I could beat it away from the rooster now. He was just too close.

Squ-wak, said the rooster again. And he fell flat at Tom's feet, just missing landing on Tom's old black tennis shoe. There was a perfectly round hole shot right through the bird's thick naked neck.

Tom looked at me wide-eyed. "Oops," he said.

"I don't think you'll be needing a scope from your uncle after all," I said. "I think all our practice done you good."

We backed out of Mrs. Comer's yard real quiet, then walked our bikes to Tom's house, shaking like two autumn leaves.

"Leah," said Tom, "Leah. I killed something. And it could have been anything or anyone." Sweat broke out above Tom's upper lip. "What if I had shot one of the twins? Or Mrs. Comer herself?"

I looked at Tom. Playing with the gun had been just a game. Trying to scare Mrs. Comer's rooster was a game too. I went cold with the thought of maybe hurting a person. I had never realized just how dangerous playing with a gun was. My hands got clammy. I wiped them on my shorts but it didn't seem to help. I felt sick to my stomach. We could have hurt someone.

Tom was so sad and sick and scared about killing Mrs. Comer's rooster that I thought he was gonna start crying. He never did in front of me. He just walked real solemn and quiet to where his daddy was sitting on their front porch and handed him the gun.

"Good-bye," he said to me, without even looking back.

I pushed away on my bike and pedaled slow past

Grandma's place. I could see Uncle Wing standing in their living room. He was talking to Papa, who was sitting in an easy chair with his casted leg propped onto the coffee table. Uncle Wing was gesturing his hands like crazy. I wondered if he was talking about another invention. Papa was nodding his head a lot. Grandma walked past the large picture window and looked right at me, but she couldn't see me because it was so bright in her place and dark where I was riding. I waved anyway.

I rode toward home. Mrs. Comer's back porch light was on. I could see her in the yard. I didn't want to look, but I did. I parked my bike in our detached garage and hid behind the hibiscus hedge, not too far from where the old rooster had chased us earlier that evening, and watched.

The red and pink and marble-colored hibiscus flowers were closed tight. I plucked two out of their green beds and sucked the sweet flavor out of the ends, hoping to calm my stomach.

I could see the rooster where he lay, a black lump. The circle of light cast from Mrs. Comer's yellow porch bulb just barely touched his claws.

I knew when Mrs. Comer saw the rooster. Her back stiffened for a second; then she leaned over real slow. She reached out her foot and with the toe of her shoe prodded the bird. I saw feathers ruffle with a small gust of wind.

Mrs. Comer squatted over a little more and

picked up her rooster. Without meaning to, I pushed through the hedge and ran across the small bit of lawn that separated us. Mrs. Comer turned to me with a start.

"Somebody's killed my rooster," she said, extending him to me as if he were a present. His head swung back and forth. One eye glared at me.

"I know," I said. "It was me. I did it with Tom. It was an accident. We didn't mean to. We were only trying to give him a little scare, and we accidentally shot him." I felt tears spring to my eyes watching this lonely old lady carry her rooster toward her house. "Do you want me to get a shovel and bury him for you?" I said.

"Goodness me, no, Leah," she said. Then she started to laugh. "This old bird isn't worth burying. He damn near drove me crazy with all his crowing. I been just waiting for him to die. I was hoping for a stray bolt of lightning, but a bullet clean through his neck? I couldn't have prayed it better. I'm plucking this old thing tonight and setting him to boil. Maybe in three days he'll be tender enough to eat." Then she laughed again and looked at me like I was silly for wanting to bury the meanest rooster in all of New Smyrna and walked into the house, flipping out the light. I stood in the dark for a minute, sniffing the chickens and gardenias and blooming peach and pear trees. Then I went home.

The next day Tom and I were invited for dinner at Mrs. Comer's house for chicken pot pie, but neither of us could go. We had looked that old booger in the eye one too many times.

June

JOHN WAYNE'S FIRST LOVE

June was so hot I thought sure I'd melt, but Uncle Wing said no, I didn't need to worry about that. He said only sweet things melt in the heat. Then he rubbed my head so hard that my hair stuck out crazy all around. It's nice to feel loved.

Outside, it was so humid I could feel the air. It was like walking through a thick cloud. Water and sweat would bead up on me just going to get the mail out of our old mailbox.

As uncomfortable as the weather sounded, I loved it. I liked sweating. I liked my clothes sticking to me. I liked the sun broiling my skin. I guess, summing it all up, I just loved the summers here in Florida.

But poor ol' Papa. He was constantly scratching under his leg cast with a wire coat hanger, even though we warned him not to. He said he was old enough to make his own decisions, and he wanted us to leave him alone. Six weeks wouldn't pass fast enough for him. He was miserable.

The second week of June Papa crutched over to the hospital. It was time for the cast to come off. Two days later Momma and Daddy decided to take a weekend jaunt up the coast to St. Augustine. Papa and I were sitting at the table in the dining room having dinner with them when Daddy broke the news to us.

"Your momma and I, we're going to have a mini-honeymoon," he said. We were all eating fried chicken. It had taken me awhile to be able even to look at chicken since the incident on Uncle Wing's fishing boat. Now I could look at it and even smell it cooking without getting sick to my stomach. I was glad about that. I always loved Momma's fried chicken.

Momma smiled kind of funny across the table at me. "We need to get away," she said.

"Get away from what?" I said. I was starting to get this feeling in the pit of my stomach. It was different from the sick one. It was like a hard knot. "Get away from who? Me?"

"Nooo," Momma and Daddy and even Papa said, singing the answer like a chorus.

"Just away," Momma said. "Not from anybody. Not really from anything."

I nodded my head at her and dug into my mashed potatoes. Brown gravy and butter broke free from the mound and slid out into my okra. The little pink ring of flowers on my plate ran around and around, pretty as could be.

"Anyway," Daddy said, playing in his peas with his fork. He cleared his throat. "Anyway. We'll be leaving tonight. Soon as we pack, right after dinner."

"That's pretty soon," I said. I was feeling very disagreeable. The feeling in my stomach was starting to feel heavy and thick, like the humidity. "Hmm." I cleared my throat.

"Course, Papa will be here with you," Momma said.

"Course," me and Papa said together.

I followed Momma around the house as she packed up her and Daddy's little suitcase. I kept wanting to reach out and touch the hem of her dress with the tips of my fingers, like I used to do when I was a little girl. I kept wanting her to sit down on their neatly made flowered bedspread and hold me on her lap. I knew I couldn't ask her to do that though. If I did, Momma for sure would call off the trip. And she herself had said they needed to get away. I kept trying to figure out my feelings. Why did it seem like there was a heavy blanket on me making it hard to breathe? I kept thinking that maybe I was sad and scared all of a sudden because Momma and Daddy were going to be gone and I wasn't going to be able to look out for them.

I walked Momma and Daddy out to our old Chevy. The sky was dark blue now. Tiny pinpoints of stars were starting to appear. The moon was already rising low in the sky, beginning its journey across the heavens.

They're leaving right now, I thought, the weight sitting like a rock in my stomach. I was sad and angry. I didn't try to talk them out of going. I knew that it wouldn't do any good. Somehow I knew even if I had gone to St. Augustine with them, this yucky feeling wouldn't go away.

Papa and I waved Momma and Daddy gone till the red taillights of the car curved around the road and disappeared. Then we went inside and watched the late show and then the late late show together. Papa went to sleep on the sofa. He was lying there, exactly like Kelly did when she was alive, both feet on the cushions. One arm was slung over his eyes, like he was shielding them from the lights of the television set. I was tired out, but I couldn't sleep.

Papa was snoring louder and louder. Suddenly he awakened himself with a big snuff. He looked confused, almost surprised. He glanced at me, then around the room. He stood and teetered for a second in his sleepiness. Then he walked over to me and kissed the top of my head.

"You and Kelly don't stay up too much longer," he said. Then he made his way to the stairs. He'd gone up three of them when he stopped.

"I'm sorry," he said. "I don't know what I was saying. I guess I had a dream about before."

I nodded at him, my mouth all dry. I was trying to swallow, but I couldn't because suddenly I knew why I was so upset. I knew why Momma and Daddy's going bothered me so much.

They were doing things without Kelly. Momma and Daddy were going to go and have a good time even though Kelly was gone. I turned off the TV and went to bed.

The next morning Papa poked me awake. "Come on downstairs," he said. "I got breakfast waiting for ya." He was smiling big into my face. He had already shaved, and his skin was smooth and brown. Wrinkles crinkled up near his eyes. I lay in the bed looking up at my grandfather. I tested my stomach to see if the rock was still there by moving my muscles like a belly dancer. It was gone. I hugged Papa tight.

Papa wasn't kidding about breakfast. He had cooked me up two popeyes and sausage and cut me a huge grapefruit in half. Sugar was sprinkled heavily on the pink pulp. A popeye is a piece of bread that has a hole cut into it. It's buttered real good on both sides and set into a frying pan. Before the butter even has a chance to start to melt, you crack an egg into the hole and cook one side. Real careful you flip that over so you don't break the yellow, and brown it on the other side. Mmm, yummy.

"I got me a plan," Papa said. He was slurping coffee from a big gray cup that said THE WORLD'S

GREATEST GRANDPA on it. There was a hair-size crack running down one side of it, and the handle had been broken and glued on twice before.

"What's that, Papa?" I said. I was poking the yellows of my eggs with my fork so they wouldn't get all hard. The only way to eat eggs is with a runny yolk. I started eating the sausage.

"How would you like to see a movie this afternoon?"

I nodded. I cut into my popeye, and the yolk ran yellow over the plain white plate. I mopped it up with part of the bread and ate a big bite.

"I was thinking that we could go and borrow your grandmother's car and take us a little drive." Papa sat back with a satisfied look on his face. "Wing won't mind getting the car for us, you know. We could just drop him off at the bridge and let him do some crabbing. He's been asking me to go crabbing with him for a while now. I checked the paper last night and the tide should be just right a little later on. We could pick him up after we've enjoyed us a nice picture show."

"Papa," I said. I was feeling sad again. These are the kinds of things I used to try to talk Kelly into doing. "Papa. You remember what they told you down at the jail. You know what would happen if they caught you driving again."

"By the grab, Leah," he said, smacking his hands together with a sharp clap. "I for sure wasn't planning on breaking the law." His green eyes were twinkling. "I was thinking that maybe I could teach you how to drive."

"No, Papa," I said. "I just can't." I don't know why Papa was thinking he needed to teach me to drive. I've been driving good for a long time now and he knows that. Before Kelly died, he was giving us both lessons on our half-acre backyard.

"Then I'll drive us around," said Papa. "I'm feeling like a trip to the movies, and I don't feel like taking the bus. It's too pretty a day."

Papa was right. Sometimes, in Florida, on Adeline Street, you wake up feeling like the world is fresh and good. That's how it was for me. I had this feeling that things were going to be okay and I was gonna make it.

Outside, it was burning hot and not even noon. The air was thick with moisture. Our house was beginning to warm up. Me and Papa had thrown open all the windows after turning off the air-conditioning right after Momma and Daddy left. We don't like to use the cooler unless it gets real hot, and I couldn't see that happening until July. There was no breeze at all. The curtains didn't puff out at the windows, not even a little bit.

After a few more slurps of coffee Papa got up and called Uncle Wing from the kitchen phone. He laughed and talked loud for a few minutes; then he lowered his voice to a loud whisper. I could hear every word he was saying. I could see him from where I was sitting too. He was looking real serious.

"Now, Wing," he said, "I got myself a little bit of a predicament. . . . Well, I was sure hoping that you'd ask that." Papa laughed. "Me and my sweet girl here wanna get outa the house. But my ol' bones are feeling too cranky to ride the bus." Papa paused, then laughed again. "Thanks, Wing. You know how to make an old man feel even older.

"This is what I was thinking. I know how you were wanting to see if you couldn't do a little crab-bin' offen the bridge. I thought maybe you could get Maude's car and we could drop you off, then go driving around for a while. I kinda wanted to go to the old Rocking Chair Plaza. *True Grit* is playing." Every Tuesday the Rocking Chair Plaza plays old movies. "Do you think Maude will go for it?"

My grandmother on my father's side does not look like a Maude. She is very prim and proper. I have never seen her without her makeup on. She is always dressed perfectly too. The only thing that looks like her name, Maude, is her wrinkles. She has a lot of wrinkles.

"Yeah, Wing, we could use your truck, but I don't like the idea of pulling your boat all over town. Too hard to park."

Uncle Wing's boat trailer is permanently attached to his truck. Don't ask me how, it just is. I have no idea how he manages to pass state inspection, but he does year after year.

"Thanks, Wing," Papa said. "We'll be seeing you."

Papa turned to me, grinning. "Looks like we'll have us a car for a little while today. Let's get these dishes washed up and get ourselves ready."

About an hour later I heard the horn from Grandma's car. She has a brand-new silver blue Cadillac Seville that Uncle Wing bought her with money from his last invention. Daddy says he paid cash. I don't know what the big deal was, but Momma seemed pretty impressed.

I looked out the window just as the car was turning into the driveway. The sun glinted off the windshield. Before it was even halfway down the drive, the passenger door slung open and Uncle Wing leaped from the car. He ran up to the porch, racing Grandma, took the stairs two at a time and ran into the house without even knocking.

"Momma's going with us," Uncle Wing said. "She wants us to drop her off for a perm-nant. I told her that we were all gonna go crabbin' off the bridge for a coupla hours. So you'll need to get some gear. We can leave it in the trunk."

Grandma knocked on the screen door, then let herself in.

"Good afternoon," she said, nodding to Papa. She looked suspiciously at Uncle Wing. "I thought sure you were gonna bust a gut running in here like that.

That's the first exercise I think I have ever seen you do."

Uncle Wing grinned, showing his fine white teeth. Then he kissed Grandma with a loud smack. She waved him away with a perfectly polished hand, her long fingernails flashing a bright pink.

Grandma is exactly opposite Uncle Wing. Where he's all sloppy and has an I-don't-care-what-you-think attitude, Grandma is spit-and-shine perfect. Her long hair is snow white and has been forever, she says. She refuses to color it. Her fingernails are an inch long and they're hers. She goes to a health spa where she works out on weights and gets a back massage three times a week. She eats healthy foods. She has even tried yoga. It's funny how two people who are so close in living ways can be so different. Kind of the way Kelly and I were. You know, her being so good and me being, well, not bad but definitely not always doing what Momma and Daddy asked.

"Thank you, Maude, for taking us around today," Papa said so properly I thought he was going to bow. "I know you're a busy woman."

Grandma sniffed. She and Papa are always real careful around each other. Momma says it's because of herself and Daddy. Don't ask me what that means. I think that they are all wonderful.

"Wing's taking you around. Not me." Then she walked over to where I was sitting, feeling guilty and excited both at once, and hugged me. "Let's go," she said. "I don't want to miss my appointment." Grandma touched the bun on top of her head and tucked a loose strand of hair back in with one long nail.

We all ran out to the car, except for Grandma, who walked out without even one nervous twitch.

"The crab cages," Uncle Wing said. He was whispering through clinched teeth. "Go get the crab cages."

Papa loped to the backyard, where he pulled our gear out from under the house. He loped back to us. The metal triangular cages clashed and clanked together. Papa had a funny look on his face. The same one Uncle Wing had. *Ha!* I thought. I never felt that uncomfortable when I was doing anything wrong. Unless, of course, I got caught. I giggled in the backseat, and Grandma turned around and looked at me.

"What are those two up to?" she said. She didn't wait for an answer but turned the air-conditioning up to high. The cool air came out of individual cooler things in the back. I adjusted mine away from me.

We dropped Grandma off in a very ritzy hair and nail salon in the new part of New Smyrna. It was painted all colors of pink and gray. There was a huge pair of scissors etched into the front pane of glass and a sign that said SHEAR PERFECTION . . . BY

APPOINTMENT ONLY. I walked Grandma to the door and kissed her good-bye. A burst of cold air and the smell of chemicals rushed out at me as a girl with purple hair walked out to where Grandma was standing.

"Mrs. Orton," she said. "Come on in." She took Grandma by one arm and led her into the building.

"Be back in three hours," Grandma said, waving her shiny nails at me. "I don't want to have to wait here all day."

Papa and I dropped Uncle Wing off at the bridge, which was already lined with fishermen. As soon as he was out of the car, we turned off the AC and rolled down the windows, all four of them, with the power box on Papa's door. Then we left Uncle Wing, his bait bucket full of chicken necks, and all five crab cages on the sidewalk, and zoomed off. The heat of the day shimmered up between us and Uncle Wing, who grew smaller and smaller, until he was just a blue speck. We turned the corner and headed off down toward the theater in the old part of town.

Papa wasn't used to the power steering and power brakes and power go that Grandma's car had. He stopped so fast and so hard and took off so fast and squealed around so many corners that I thought I might bite my tongue off. I laughed every time at first, but pretty soon I had an ache in my neck, and it wasn't funny anymore.

We were probably only a half mile from the theater when I noticed Mrs. Comer. She was walking alongside the road, down the sidewalk, pulling her big old red wagon.

Lots of times when Mrs. Comer goes walking, she pulls her wagon. She's not a bag lady by any means. But sometimes she stops at the store and buys a few groceries or goes to the library and gets a dozen books. She's too old to carry things a long way, and since she never learned to drive, she takes her wagon. Momma did try to teach Mrs. Comer to drive last year before Kelly died. But it wasn't a big success. Mrs. Comer ran into our clothesline pole and knocked out a headlight. She only got the one lesson.

Today, I thought, she was awfully far from home. When we passed her, I could see her wagon was empty.

"Papa," I said, "that's Mrs. Comer."

"Sure is," Papa said. He beeped and waved. Mrs. Comer looked up, startled. She didn't recognize us.

"Stop, Papa," I said. "I think she's confused. She's too far from home. We need to pick her up."

Papa slowed the car but didn't stop.

"We can't take her home and make it back in time for the movie," Papa said. "I think she's gonna be okay. She didn't know who we are because of this fancy car." Papa jerked the car to a stop at a red light, like he was proving to me that it was the car that had fooled Mrs. Comer. But I knew better.

"No, Papa," I said. "She might get hurt. We gotta take care of her. Let's just take her to the show with us. Then we can make sure she gets home safe."

"And what's your grandmother gonna say about Rose Comer in her car with a wagon?" Papa had edged the car over to the curb and parked in front of a yellow fire hydrant.

"What's Grandma gonna say about you driving her car, wagon or no wagon?" I said, climbing out. I walked to Mrs. Comer. Papa backed up along the road beside me.

"I went for snuff," she said when I got close to her. "And now I'm lost." I thought for a second she was going to cry, but she didn't.

"Come with us to the show," I said. "We're going to see *True Grit*." I touched her arm.

"I love grits with sugar," she said, with a far-off look in her eyes.

"No," I said. "*True Grit* is a John Wayne movie. We're going there right now. Papa and I want you to come."

"Oh," said Mrs. Comer, suddenly irritated. She thrust her finger at the window where Papa had poked his head out my side of the car. He looked irritated too. He checked his watch, obviously. "Will *he* be there?" she said.

"Yes, Mrs. Comer. He's driving us and then paying." Mrs. Comer sniffed but walked to the car, pulling her wagon. The wheels squeaked all the way to the rear of the car.

Papa jumped out to help Mrs. Comer and her wagon in. He was pushing her to the back door, trying to make her hurry. Finally she jerked her arm free from him and said between clinched teeth, "I've already memorized your tag number, you old geezer. I could give any policeman a complete description of you. I could have you locked up that fast." Mrs. Comer snapped her fingers under Papa's nose. It was obvious that Mrs. Comer didn't recognize Papa. I was pretty sure she knew who I was.

"Get in the car, Rose," said Papa with a sigh. "We're gonna miss the beginning of the movie, and I hate to miss the beginning." Papa was not happy. He was growling.

Mrs. Comer allowed herself to be guided into the back of the car. Papa put the wagon in the trunk. Then he jumped behind the steering wheel.

"Four minutes," he said, glancing at the digital clock on the dashboard. Then we were off. Up and over the curb, narrowly missing the fire hydrant. We squealed, jerked, shot off, and slammed to a stop over and over again until we were finally at the Rocking Chair Plaza.

This theater seems as old as the fort. It's squished between Leon's diner and a tiny shoe repair shop. It is so old that the antique air-conditioning unit is always breaking down. That means in the summer you usually sweat every ounce of fat off your body while watching movies. That's one of the reasons Papa and I like the Rocking Chair so much. You know, because it's nice and hot. That and the fact that it's the cheapest place in town to see a movie. Only ninety-nine cents.

Today, again, the air-conditioning was off. We walked into the dark room, filled with comfortable chairs that rocked, guiding Mrs. Comer between us. She stumbled on the sloping floor. Already the air was hot. At each of the four doors a large fan hummed and blew the hot smells of popcorn and people around the room. The heavy mauve curtains pulled to the sides of the large screen waved gently.

There were only seven other people there to watch the movie. I was the only person under fifty. Papa walked quickly to his favorite seat, one he swears is in the very center of the theater, and sat down. The previews were blasting the news of coming attractions. There was one that looked pretty funny, with Billy Crystal as the star. I sat beside Papa, then pulled Mrs. Comer into the chair on the other side of me.

As soon as John Wayne appeared on the screen, Mrs. Comer leaped to her feet.

"I know that man," she screeched. "I've seen him on the eleven o'clock news. Isn't he a murderer?" The flowers on her dress swayed with the same emotion Mrs. Comer was shouting with. "I think we should call the police. I am sure I have seen that face on *America's Most Wanted.*"

"Make her sit down and shut up," Papa said.

"Mrs. Comer," I said, touching her arm softly. She sat down beside me and looked, concerned, into my face. Her eyes were magnified to a huge owl size behind her glasses. "Mrs. Comer. That's John Wayne. He's a famous movie star."

"John Wayne?" Mrs. Comer said. "John Wayne?" She settled back into her chair and rocked hard three or four times. "I know him. Why, that's John Wayne." She clutched my arm, her bony fingers pressing into my flesh. "Did you know that I went on a carriage ride with him?"

Mrs. Comer's loud whisper floated over to Papa, who batted it back with "We practically stole a car to get to see this movie, and now I'm having to lip-read. Rose, be quiet. Please." He sat back with a snap.

"Use a softer voice, Mrs. Comer. There are people here trying to watch the show."

"There are?" Mrs. Comer craned her neck around. Her hair looked blue from the movie lights. "I thought we were the only people in here. I thought it was just you and me and that old coot." Mrs. Comer jerked her head toward Papa, who raised his top lip into an ugly sneer.

Mrs. Comer settled back and smiled adoringly at John Wayne.

"Isn't he handsome?" she said to me. It was so soft I could barely hear her.

"Yeah," I said. And I believed it too. He was handsome for an old man. Nearly as good-looking as Tom. For a moment I imagined how it would be watching the movie with Tom. My face turned pink at the thought.

"Why, it's as hot as Hades in here," Mrs. Comer said, and took off her sweater.

"Hush," said Papa through gritted teeth. Mrs. Comer was right though. It was hot. Hotter than usual. The fans droned like huge bees. The curtains waved. I sweated. My T-shirt started sticking to me under my arms.

Mrs. Comer quieted down, and we all watched John Wayne. This old movie captured me. Sure, it was a little corny, you know the stunt stuff. But it was better than lots of things that I've seen lately on TV. It was almost real.

The room became warmer and warmer. I sat forward, my chin resting on my damp hands, my elbows propped on my knees. Next to me Mrs. Comer wriggled in the heat. I was glad that I had on just a light T-shirt and shorts and sandals. I was double glad that my hair was pulled back into a ponytail and not hanging in and sticking to my face.

I wiped the sweat from my forehead. This was like being in a sauna, dripping wet and very hot. I wondered vaguely what the temperature was outside.

"I know what hell is like now," said Mrs. Comer. She waved a popcorn box she had picked up off the floor around in the air. It didn't help any. The seat was itchy under my legs.

Papa grunted. I wiped more sweat away.

"Now I know what it's like to be burned to death," said Mrs. Comer, a little louder this time.

I nodded. It was quiet for a little while. I think I remember Mrs. Comer muttering that the only way to be comfortable in such a scalding heat was to be completely naked. She was right. She wriggled some more and mumbled about how it had been rather hot the day she took that carriage ride with John Wayne.

John Wayne was shooting all the bad guys and I was sweating and Mrs. Comer was wriggling. Papa was saying lots of the lines from the movie under his breath. He always does that.

"The fires of hell couldn't be hotter than the air in this room," Mrs. Comer hollered at the back of my head. "I'm taking a nap."

"Okay," I said. Pretty soon I could hear her snoring.

Then John Wayne was righting all the world's wrongs and finally walking into a perfect sunset. The lights flicked on, and I sighed. Yes, I decided right then, John Wayne was a real hero.

I stood up and stretched. I turned, my arms still

in the air. I looked at Papa, who was rubbing his eyes. Then I looked at Mrs. Comer.

There she was, sitting there, nearly naked. Mrs. Comer's clothes were spread around her, on the chair beside her, on the floor. Even on the back of my chair. How had her slip gotten there? Had I sat forward the whole show? Her mouth was open and her false teeth were loose in her mouth. That must have been why she was snoring earlier. But she wasn't snoring now. In the dim lights of the sweltering theater, I was sure Mrs. Comer was dead.

I screamed. Papa jumped to his feet.

"What in the world," Papa said, jerking his head from Mrs. Comer's white, nearly naked body to me standing dumbfounded and scared, then back again to Mrs. Comer.

"She's dead." I said right in Papa's ear. He was trying to get past me to Mrs. Comer. "She's dead from the heat." I couldn't believe it.

The people we had shared the theater with walked down to where we were. A movie attendant with a flashlight and one with a small broom and garbage bag ran to call 911.

I leaned forward and took Mrs. Comer's flowered cotton dress and laid it over her white, wrinkled body, covering her beige underwear and bra. The smell of lilacs became strong as I leaned close to her.

"Rose," Papa said. "Rose." He had this funny

look on his face. Almost like he was going to laugh at our naked, dead neighbor. Papa turned to me.

There was a loud noise, and three men came running down the aisle.

"Let us in here," one of them said, elbowing his way past the onlookers. He had a dark brown, thin line of a mustache. He knelt in front of Mrs. Comer, then took her wrist into his hand.

Mrs. Comer leaned forward, startling us all, and slapped the man who held her arm. One of the moviegoers screamed.

"John," she said, "I don't care how big of a star you are. I'm a lady. You can't have your way with me. Now get these horses going and take me home." The 911 man's mouth dropped open. Papa giggled.

When everybody left, I helped Mrs. Comer get dressed. The second movie was delayed because of us. A small crowd was waiting when we stepped out into the bright June sunlight. Everyone started whispering.

"That's the old lady we all thought was dead," said an attendant. We pushed our way through the people and finally into the car.

Papa laughed all over New Smyrna.

When we got home, I hustled Mrs. Comer to her place. A little bit later I brought her a plate of food that Papa had prepared. It wasn't until after our late lunch that Papa remembered we had forgotten

Grandma and Uncle Wing. We raced the back way to the bridge.

About a mile from where we had left him, we found Uncle Wing. He had a bucketful of crabs in one hand, and he was carrying a lot of gear in the other. There was some even tied around his shoulders. He was real mad. His old fishing hat was bent funny from where he had fanned himself with it. His face and his arms were sunburned a bright pink.

On the way to pick up Grandma we passed the bank. The sign said it was 108 degrees. No wonder it had been so hot in the theater.

Uncle Wing grumbled all the way to the salon. But Grandma was so busy talking to the girl with the purple hair she didn't even notice we were an hour late. Her fingernails were orange now. I bet her toenails matched. Her hair was wavy in its bun.

At dinnertime Papa and I ate in silence. Every once in a while Papa would start laughing, first his belly shaking soft so I wouldn't know, then his shoulders, and finally his head. He never smiled even once. But he couldn't fool me. I knew he was laughing.

I was sure I didn't think it was funny. In fact, seeing Mrs. Comer practically naked and so wrinkled was sad to me.

And so was a discovery I had made.

I had had a good time without Kelly. I thought about it all during dinner and then in bed. I remembered all the times I had done something alone, without my sister, and had fun. There were getting to be more and more of those good times. And I wasn't sure that I liked it.

I had to keep on living. Sometimes sad, sometimes lonely. Sometimes laughing my guts out. Always without Kelly. Even if I didn't like it or want to, I had to keep on living.

You know the weirdest part of this finding out?

It was that I was sad. And that I was glad.

Suddenly I started laughing about what had happened that day. Laughing at Mrs. Comer, white and wrinkled and naked in the hot Rocking Chair Plaza. I laughed so hard Papa came into my room to find out what the matter was. I laughed until my side ached and the tears ran out of my eyes.

"What? What?" Papa asked over and over again.

"Mrs. Comer," I finally wheezed out.

Then Papa was laughing with me. We laughed and screeched and told the story over and over again until I thought I'd bust wide open. Then we went downstairs and each had a piece of apple pie that Momma had left for us. With ice cream.

July

VICKIE

In July Momma started acting really funny. I don't mean funny ha-ha either. I mean funny strange.

First, at the end of June she made it perfectly clear that we would not be traveling up to the family reunion. My eyes nearly popped out of my head when Momma told us that. In all my almost thirteen years we had never missed a reunion. Not even when Randy, my second cousin, was wanted by the police for a 7-Eleven robbery. We all met in Daytona that year, and in the middle of singing the police arrived and carried him off. I remember that like it was yesterday and I wasn't but six or so. We all stood on the curb of Great-Aunt Mamie's house and waved good-bye. He grinned at us from the rear window of the police car.

This year it was to be at Cousin Lissie's place in Waycross, Georgia. She had married Myron, the man she brought to last year's reunion. They had bought a new house and insisted the reunion be at their place. Uncle Wing, still mad because of the one and only time Kelly and I listened to Cousin Lissie about frogs giving you warts, said it was because our cousin wanted to show off that she could finally get married.

When I asked Momma why we weren't going to go, she said she was too tired.

Momma too tired? Momma has always been the last to go to bed and the first up in the morning. She's always the longest shopper and the first person at the Saturday morning garage sales. In all my life I have never heard Momma complain that she was too tired to do anything. But with July's incredible heat and mugginess came Momma crawling slow motion everywhere she went. If she went.

And there was one more thing I thought was kind of funny about Momma: Daddy. Daddy was always hanging over her. Momma would complain of the heat, and Daddy would run and turn down the thermostat, practically chasing Papa and me from our very own house. I had to sleep with a blanket at night.

Momma would mention that she was feeling a bit thirsty, and Daddy would run to the kitchen and mix up a big pitcher of freshly brewed iced tea. Momma would say she was feeling a bit uncomfortable, and Daddy would rearrange the sofa pillows, tucking them under her feet and behind her back. Momma would complain about skinning raw chicken and how it made her feel like throwing up, and Daddy would heat up the grill. Yes! It was really happening. My daddy started cooking most of the meals. It was all very un-Orton-like.

Talking to Papa made me sure there was something kooky with my family.

"What's wrong with them?" I whispered to Papa when Daddy went over to readjust the brightness on the TV for Momma.

Papa smiled crookedlike and whispered back, "They're in love."

"In love?" I said. "They're weird."

Another strange thing happened in July. Tom and his family went up North to visit relatives and I began visiting with Vickie.

I guess until I started really being friends with Vickie, I figured families were like my own. You know. There was a mom and dad and maybe a brother and a sister. And everybody in the family loved each other.

That's not to say that all the families in New Smyrna Beach, Florida, are happy. Two of my aunts got divorced years ago. There are lots of kids in my school whose parents are divorced. In fact, there is this one girl in the fifth grade, Angel Brown, whose mom has been married six times.

But all these parents love their kids. I mean, that's the way it's supposed to be. A mom and a dad have a kid and they love it.

In July I found out that is not always true.

Vickie's house is a tiny log cabin set way out past

the animal shelter. It has only one bedroom that her mom shares with Vickie's little sister. The screened-in back porch is where Vickie sleeps.

All July either Vickie was at my place or we were riding our bikes. Whenever I came to pick her up, she'd run out before I'd even had a chance to coast down the driveway. It was like she sat waiting for me. She'd come out the door, making sure it closed quietlike behind her, then jump on her bike and pedal to meet me.

"Hey," she said. It was a Saturday morning, and I had called her early because Momma and Daddy were going shopping together for groceries. Daddy grocery shopping! It was enough to make you snort with disgust. Daddy hates any kind of shopping. "Guess what? My mom says you can spend the night tonight if you want to."

I looked toward the cabin. I had met Vickie's mom only one time before when she had dropped Vickie off at my house for a sleepover. She hadn't seemed really happy. And Vickie had been red-eyed. When I tried to find out what she had been crying for, Vickie refused to talk about it. I didn't know if I could spend the night with her. For some reason I was a little scared of her mom. Or maybe it was just scared of being in a strange place overnight. I hadn't been to anybody's house since Kelly died. Not even over to Grandma's and Uncle Wing's place all night.

"You wanna come?" Vickie looked at me wide-eyed. "We went to the store yesterday and bought lots of treats. We could get up in the middle of the night and raid the kitchen. We could watch videos all night. We just got a VCR. What do you think? Do you think your mom and dad would let you?"

I shrugged my shoulders. "Probably," I said.

"Come on," Vickie said, grabbing my arm. Her hand was cool and tanned. "It'd be fun. Please."

"Let me talk to my mother," I said. "Let's go exploring now. Did you pack a lunch?"

Vickie nodded and ran into the house. She came back swinging a brown paper sack. She got her bike and we started off.

The west side of New Smyrna, the part of the city farthest from the beach, is full of new construction. The woods are being torn down and replaced with new housing projects and condominiums. Just past this is a terrific place for exploring.

Oak trees years old grow crowded. Palm trees and palm fronds are squished together. Laced in and out and among all this are miles of streams. Some wide and deep and green. Other shallow and yellow-colored. All of them fast-moving and exciting because there is nothing around except the whispering wind and frogs and animal tracks.

Tom and I accidentally discovered this place right after the killing of Mrs. Comer's rooster. But we hadn't had the chance to come out and see what all was going on here. We'd planned on taking a few days to explore and make maps of the waterways and maybe even take his two-man boat down a few of the bigger streams. Then Tom's dad, Mr. Blandford, decided he needed to take a vacation from making keys. He hired somebody to take his place the month of July, and they were off. Before they left, Tom came over to tell me good-bye.

"Listen, Leah," he said, touching my hand just barely with two fingers, "it's okay by me if you go on out to the woods and explore without me." He smiled real sadlike because it was such a hard thing to say.

"Only if I get bored outa my head, Tom," I said, my heart thumping so I wondered if he could hear it. Tom had touched my hand a million times before, when we were climbing trees or digging through the dump or arm wrestling. Did he notice a difference, or was it just me?

Well, it wasn't boredom that drove me to go exploring without Tom but Momma and her new ways.

Vickie and I traveled up the road toward the new construction sites. The late-morning sun was beating down hard and hot. Sweat rolled down my face, leaving cool stripes and curly hair around my face. The still, heavy air moved only when a car or truck zoomed past us on the road. We hadn't been pedaling long when I started wishing for a big cold drink.

I was glad that I had a can of pop in the pack tied to my bike.

It took us forty-five minutes to get to the first stream. We got off our bikes and pushed through the low undergrowth and finally into the sea of trees and bushes.

"Wow," I said. "It sure is hot."

"Yeah," said Vickie, smoothing her hair back from her face with one hand. "But it's great to be out here, don't you think?" She breathed in deep and let the air out slowly.

"Yeah," I said. I looked out at the stream. It was just wide enough to make a good jumping width. The sand along its edges was white, like the ocean sand. It looked a bit deep. I mean, deep enough to wade and sit and maybe even float around in a while. I slipped off one tennis shoe and sock and touched the water with my foot. Yup, it was a cool stream. "Can you swim?" I said to Vickie.

"Course," she said to me. Then she grinned.

I grinned back at her.

"Do you want to swim?" I was already taking off my other shoe.

"Course," Vickie. She was taking off her shoes, too.

We waded out into the stream water. It flowed cool and sweet past my ankles toward what? The ocean? Maybe.

One of the wonderful things about Florida is that

it is filled with plenty of spring-fed lakes and streams. I kept on thinking that maybe if we followed the flow of this one, we might be able to find a hidden lake, unknown to anyone. Maybe even the Fountain of Youth that Ponce de León searched for. I wondered for a second what the Fountain of Youth could do for someone who was already dead; then I forced myself not to think about it anymore.

Butterflies zigzagged, and dragonflies dodged about. Frogs were singing a rain song, begging for moisture.

"Let's follow this and see where we end up," said Vickie.

We left our shoes and bicycles on the streambed ledge and started off with our lunches. The stream widened and narrowed as we walked. Trees crowded close, leaning over the water, then opened up wide, allowing the burning sun in. Mosquitoes buzzed and bit, and gnats tried to fly into our noses.

We kept wandering, and then, like something from a movie, we pushed through one more dense area of palm fronds and tree branches and were there.

Our stream rushed downhill about twenty feet, making a tiny, fast-flowing waterfall. Grasses grew thick in the water at the top; then only rushing water slid toward a water hole, too small to be a lake. It was about the size of a small swimming pool. The water bubbled there, feeding into this pool along with two other streams. Then the pond broke open and flowed off into four different directions.

"Oh, my gosh," said Vickie. "Will you look at that? It's just beautiful."

"Let's go down the fall," I said. I sat down. The water rushed around my hips, pounding on my middle back, splashing up on my T-shirt, making dark blue circles appear on the light blue material. I sat for a second, hesitating. The water was cold and fast.

I had once heard about a boy who went swimming in a lake in Longwood, Florida. He was splashing around, having a good time, when a swarm of water moccasins attacked and killed him. What would be waiting in the pool below me?

"You gonna do this?" I said. Vickie was wading in behind me. She sat down, spraying the water into my hair. She didn't seem worried about snakes at all. Maybe she hadn't heard the story about the boy in Longwood.

"We'll be a train," Vickie said loud in my ear, and before I could say anything, she pushed us over the first hill, and we were rushing over the tiny falls. I wondered briefly if water moccasins would kill us both at the same time or just me because I was first. We dipped and bounced toward the pool, where the sun's reflection was shining diamond chips.

At the lip of the fall, before we hit the water, I glanced around. Tall grasses were waving us on. A red-wing blackbird was perched on a low oak limb. There was a sandy beach good enough for tanning, across from us. And there weren't any snakes that I could see.

Then the water closed over my head, and I was under, with Vickie pushing me down, then away. I touched the bottom of the pool and pushed up.

This pool was way over my head. There was a fresh spring here. If there hadn't been so many run-offs, there would have been a wonderful lake right where we were.

"Wow!" I said to Vickie. She was dog-paddling to the side, then climbing out. "Wow!" I said again.

"Let's do it some more," she said.

We spent the whole rest of the day playing and splashing in the water. We ate a late lunch. Then swam and slid. We explored this little haven, then swore that we'd tell no one of this place, except Tom, and that we'd come often.

We were sitting quiet, listening to the crickets singing an evening song, when Vickie jumped to her feet.

"We gotta go," she said, and without waiting for me to answer, she took off running up the stream. I followed behind her, calling for her to wait. But she didn't slow down. I hurried to catch up and after a little bit was running next to her, although it was nearly impossible to do because of the high weeds and grasses that grew where I had to run.

"What's wrong?" I said. "What is it? Did you see something? Was there a snake back there?"

"No," Vickie said. "I just gotta get home. I didn't realize it was this late. My momma's gonna kill me." She ran faster, and I fell in behind her, stepping in her footprints, splashing in the widening, then narrowing stream.

We had trekked in at least a mile, and when we finally came to where we had parked our bikes and left our socks and shoes, the sun was an orange disk, low in the sky, painting the clouds warm hues. But there was no time to admire sunsets.

"Oh, no," Vickie said. "Oh, no."

"What?" I said. "What?"

Vickie was forcing her feet into her tennis shoes, mud and all. I did the same, then shoved my socks into my pockets.

"I'm in a lot of trouble," she said almost to herself.

"Should I still come to your house?" I said.

Vickie looked at me.

"There's no time for me to go to your place first," she said. She threw her leg over her bicycle and started pedaling fast, toward her home. I could tell she was racing the sun. But we had a long way to go.

"What should I do?" I called to her. I pedaled fast so I could get up next to her. The road was quiet, and only a few cars passed us. The air was still, hot, and heavy. "Should I go on home? Or call my mom from your place?"

Vickie was shaking her curly hair out and fanning her shirt, trying to make them dry.

"I don't want to get you in trouble."

"Leah," she said, real matter-of-fact, "I already am in trouble. It's just hard to know how my mom's going to be when I get there." Lightning bugs were flitting around now. Frogs sang for rain and crickets played evening songs. The hot air rushed past my ears, nearly drowning out the music of the night. My legs were tired from pedaling. An ache grew in my side from going so fast. I was tired from our long day. And I was hungry too.

"I'll go with you," I said. "Maybe if I'm with you, your mom won't be so mad. I'll call my house from your place."

Vickie smiled at me briefly, and then we both concentrated on getting to her home as quickly as possible.

It was dark when we bounced down the rock driveway to the little log cabin, where few lights burned. The silhouette of the house blended in with huge trees that bent toward it. Before we had even parked the bikes, Vickie's mom was out of the house.

"Where have you been?" she said. Her voice was like ice, and I felt really cold for the first time that day, maybe even that summer.

"I'm sorry, Mother," Vickie said. "I was having so much fun that I lost track of time."

"I was worried sick," she said.

"I know, Momma, and I'm really sorry."

Vickie got off her bicycle and started forward, her hand extended to her mother, who was standing in a box of light that flooded from a large window and made the night seem darker.

"Who do you think you are, making me wait like that? Making me worry like that?" Her mother was talking through clenched teeth. Vickie stopped where she was.

"I'm sorry, Mrs. Abernathy," I said. "It's really my fault. We were playing and having a good time, and we just didn't realize how late it had become."

Mrs. Abernathy's hand flew out from her body and slapped Vickie on her chin and neck. Before I could even move, she had punched Vickie hard in the chest with her other hand. Vickie squatted down, lifting her arm up, pointing her elbow to the sky.

"I didn't mean to make you worry, Momma," she said.

One bare foot poked quickly out of the darkness, knocking Vickie into her bike. It fell over, and the back wheel spun with a buzz and a clickity-click.

"Not now, Momma," Vickie cried. But it was like her mother couldn't hear anything. Mrs. Abernathy hit and kicked her daughter, who now lay facedown on the ground.

"Stop," I cried, letting my bike fall and running to where Vickie was. I tried to pull her to her feet. To pull her closer to me. "Stop. Please. It was my fault." Mrs. Abernathy kicked and hit around me.

"Momma, nooo," said a little girl from the window.

"You make me so sick," Mrs. Abernathy wheezed. Her face was hard and set, intent on what she was doing. "I hate you. I wish you had never been born. I wish you were dead." She stared right at me then, and without meaning to, I moved away. Still, she was close enough that I could see her bottom teeth were crooked. "Get off my property and never come back."

"Vickie," I said, "come home with me. Please." I stumbled over her bike, trying to work my way back to where she was lying on the ground. Mrs. Abernathy stood between her daughter and me. I thought I heard the little girl in the window crying; then I realized it was me. "Please. My momma won't care if you call or not. Please."

"Get out of here," Vickie's mother said, again. Her voice was the same icy tone it had been when she first spoke. In fact, the whole time this was going on, she had never even raised her tone once.

My hand reached out, and I felt Vickie. She was breathing fast. I crawled over to her.

"Come with me," I whispered into the back of Vickie's head. I could smell the stream and the day in her hair. "It'll be okay. You can sleep in my room. In Kelly's bed. It won't matter that we don't call first. It won't matter that we're late."

Vickie turned her face toward me. Her eyes were so big and sad that my voice caught in my throat.

"This isn't right," I whispered.

"Leave us in peace," screamed Mrs. Abernathy.

Suddenly I was screaming too. "This isn't right. This isn't right."

I was standing now.

"Go home, Leah," said Vickie. "Go home."

"Go home," screamed her mother.

"I can't leave you," I said.

"Please. It'll be better if you go."

"What have you been telling her?" screamed Mrs. Abernathy. She grabbed Vickie's hair in both hands and pulled her to her feet. She began to drag her toward the house. Through the square of yellow light. Up the steps.

"Nothing, Momma. Nothing."

"I know you've been telling people about me. I know it. You've told everyone, haven't you?"

"No, Momma. I haven't told anyone anything. I swear it."

"Stop," I cried, climbing on my bike. "She's never told me anything about you. I'll go home if you just leave her alone."

"Good-bye, Leah," Vickie said from the steps. "Hurry."

I pushed off on the ground and started pedaling.

"Leave my property," shouted Vickie's mother, large and dark in the doorway. "Leave us in peace."

I went as fast as I could, watching the moon, huge and white, letting it guide me, crying and praying, home.

Momma and Daddy weren't home when I got there. Papa was asleep in the recliner, watching an old James Bond movie. The living room glowed blue from the television.

I crept through, past Papa, and climbed the stairs silently, taking them two at a time. I went in my room and fell on my bed. The clock said ten thirty-nine. I didn't bother turning on the light, and I didn't bother taking off my damp clothes and tennis shoes. I just lay on my stomach and thought about the things I had seen that night.

Without meaning to, I drifted off to sleep. At two-sixteen I woke up uncomfortable, with a bad taste in my mouth and a headache. At first I couldn't figure out why I was feeling so sad. Then I remembered Vickie and her mother and the little girl at the window.

I got up and looked out into the backyard. I could see our garage and part of Mrs. Comer's yard really well. I used to be able to see her rooster sitting on top of the henhouse, crowing at the moon.

Now there wasn't much light because it wasn't a very big moon. But the stars were bright. I could see the Big Dipper.

There was a slight wind blowing, and clothes on our clothesline were dancing slow and ghostlike. I wondered for a second why Momma hadn't brought them in. She was probably not feeling very good today.

I started thinking about Vickie. About her mother.

I took off my clothes and piled them in a heap next to my door. I pushed my shoes off and kicked them toward my bed. Standing in my underwear, I looked at my dark reflection in the mirror that hung inside my closet. I looked and looked at myself for a long time, trying to figure things out.

Why was Vickie's mom that way? Why was Mrs. Comer alone? Why was Kelly dead? It just seemed to me life and people and living should be like the tiny waterfall and swimming pool Vickie and I had found. You know, fast-flowing, cool, beautiful, peaceful.

Looking at myself, I suddenly got this funny feeling in the pit of my stomach. Life was beautiful. And sad. And scary. And wonderful. And lots of times horribly unfair.

I didn't like all this thinking. I didn't like this feeling. I just wanted to be a dumb kid, always living with my mother and father and grandfather in this house, with Mrs. Comer next door, with Vickie and

Tom as my best friends. Suddenly I knew it wasn't always going to be that way.

I went over and climbed into Kelly's bed. I could hardly smell her anymore. And that was sad and final, too.

I sniffed her pillow really deep, then rolled onto my side and after a while went to sleep.

August

AN END AND A BEGINNING

I didn't call Vickie after the day at our special place. I was afraid of her mother. Afraid that I might see more. For three weeks I avoided my friend.

Another thing was weighing heavy on my mind. School would be starting soon. School was how I marked the last day of Kelly's life because that was where we were going when she died.

I pushed the sad thoughts of Kelly out of my mind. And after a lot of arguing with myself I decided to go see Vickie. I was pretty sure that her mother was at the college teaching. At least I was praying that she was.

And if she wasn't? I didn't know what I'd do.

I got on my bicycle and started the long ride over to Vickie's home.

At the top of Vickie's driveway I hid my bike in the bushes. Then I walked slow down to her house.

I knocked on the old door. Brown paint was peeling from it. A cat weaved its way around my ankles, humming. I heard two voices come from inside, and my heart started fluttering. A chill went down my neck and all the way down my back. Vickie's mother was home. I had judged wrongly. I almost ran.

Vickie opened the door. Beside her stood the little girl I had seen in the window that night.

"Leah!" Vickie said, her voice high with surprise. "Leah! I thought you hated me. Why are you here? How did you get here? Can you come in?"

I nodded, then laughed. I was so relieved my head hurt.

"I came to visit. Is it okay?"

"Yes," said Vickie, grabbing my wrist. "Yes. Come in. My mother is at work. She teaches during the summer, you know. Today is her last day of classes. She's off for a week, starting tomorrow."

Vickie led me into her home. I went in through a small kitchen, down a tiny hall, through her mother's room, and out onto a screened-in porch. This was where Vickie slept. There was a dresser and a small bed. A desk and chair were pushed against one of the screened walls. There were books piled on homemade shelves. At the far end of the porch there was a door to the outside.

"Sit down," Vickie said, pointing to her bed. The little girl hugged tight to Vickie's leg. Vickie moved carefully so as not to jar her, then sat down next to me. She pulled the child onto her lap. I could see by looking at both of them that Vickie had looked exactly like this when she was little.

"This is Valerie, my sister," said Vickie. "She'll be

four in another week. Huh, Val? Valerie, this is my best friend, Leah."

Valerie gazed at me, then popped her thumb into her mouth.

"You don't have to be afraid, Valerie," said Vickie. "This is my friend." Vickie looked at me with eyes big and wide. "Right? You are my friend, aren't you, Leah? Isn't that why you came here? Or did you come to tell me that you weren't?"

"I'm your friend, Vickie," I said. "I'm your friend." I took a big breath. "And I'm worried. I'm scared for you."

Vickie's face began to color. She pulled Valerie close to her, and the little girl closed her eyes.

"There's nothing you can do," Vickie said. "This is my life."

I was real quiet for a couple of minutes. "It's wrong, Vickie. It's bad wrong."

Vickie nodded. "It's like that a lot. You know. Like when you were here before."

I sat quiet for a minute. So did Vickie. Then she said, "Listen. I don't know why things are the way they are. But my mom, she needs me. She's always telling me that. She tells me I'm her helper. I work with her to figure out the budget. I keep the house clean. I cook and do the laundry. I watch Valerie. Who would help my mom if I didn't?"

I thought about my mother. Okay, so lately she had been acting a little funny, but that wasn't really her. And even though my mom wasn't doing all the things she normally did, she was still doing a lot. In fact, my mom did all the things Vickie had to do.

"Where's your dad?" I said. "Does he know . . . what it's like here?"

Vickie sucked in a lot of air, then let it out slowly. Valerie's hair blew up softly.

"Mom told me he left. He left because of u-s," she said, spelling the last word.

"Who told you that?" I said. "Who told you he left for that reason?"

"Mom did. She said w-e drove him away from her. Valerie doesn't know. And I don't want her to. But listen, Leah. This is really personal. I've never told anyone this stuff. Not even my grandparents. No one knows things are like this. And if Mom knew I spoke to you about these things, she would be furious." Vickie was whispering now, so low I could almost not hear her. Our heads were together. I nodded to her.

"There's one more thing, Leah. My mom can really be nice too. She hits me a lot. But every once in a while she's really, really nice. And on those days we'll go out to eat as a family or she'll tell me nice things about myself. It's not all bad."

"Something has to be done," I said. "I'm sure there's someone who could help you."

"If people knew, they might take us away," Vickie

AN END AND A BEGINNING

said. "And who would help my mother then? Promise you won't tell anyone, Leah. Please."

I tried hard to make myself say what Vickie wanted to hear. I tried really hard. "I want to be your friend. But I can't promise that, Vickie. I can't."

I left a little later. It was getting close to the time for Mrs. Abernathy to come home and I didn't want to be around when she got back. The whole walk up the drive I kept imagining her coming down the driveway and seeing me there. Would she run over me with the car? She had told me to get off her property and never come back.

I pulled my bike out of the bushes and started home. I thought about all the things I would say to Mrs. Abernathy if I ever saw her again. Well, things that I might say. About how nice her daughter was and how she should be good to her own flesh-and-blood kids. But I knew that if I ever did say anything to her, things would be worse for Vickie. That was one of the things that Mrs. Abernathy seemed worried about that night, that people might know how she was. Someone else would have to talk to her. Not just some kid. And I had no idea who.

On the way home I stopped by Tom's house. He was sitting on his front porch, looking kind of down-in-the-dumps.

"Killed any chickens lately?" I said, pulling into his driveway.

Tom jumped up. "Hush, Leah," he said, waving me down with his hands. "Nobody knows anything about that here."

"You do," I said, and grinned at him.

"Don't be funny. I'm trying to forget that I know about it."

I dropped my bike in the yard and went to sit with Tom.

"Two more weeks till school starts," he said.

"I know," I said. "Tom. Did you know it's been almost a year."

He nodded.

One good thing about Tom is that he always knows what I'm talking about, even if I change the subject right in the middle of the conversation. Or start a new conversation without a warning.

"This has been the longest year of my life," I said. "I didn't think I'd ever get through it. For a while there I thought I'd always be stuck with that horrible first feeling of knowing that Kelly would never be here again. It was awful."

"Do you miss her still?" Tom said.

I turned my face into the afternoon sun. The sky was intensely blue. I couldn't see even one cloud anywhere.

"Yeah," I said. "I miss her a lot. But now I don't get all crinkled up with the pain of it. Well, not as often."

"I miss her too," Tom said. Then after a while:

"Leah? Are we still gonna be friends. You know, like we are now?" Tom looked quick down at the ground, then back up into my face.

"Yeah," I said. It was a little hard to swallow. Tom took my hand and squeezed it. He smiled suddenly.

"Let's go on over to my house," I said. "Momma won't care if you eat over."

Tom went around back to get his bicycle. I could still feel the pressure of his hand on mine. We rode the two blocks slow to my house, making crazy-eight circles in the road as we went.

When I pulled into the driveway, a funny feeling crept into my heart. It was like I was having one of Kelly's feelings. A feeling that something was wrong.

Daddy was home. Daddy is usually never home in the middle of the day. Unless, of course, there's a problem.

I drove fast up the driveway and jumped off my bike before it had stopped, letting it crash in the side yard. I could hear the wheels whirring as I ran into the sunroom, then up the stairs into the main part of the house. Tom came running behind me.

"Momma!" I yelled. "Daddy! Momma! Where are you?" I heard sounds coming from upstairs. My heart was racing. Momma! It had to be her. These weird ways she had been acting. Maybe she was sick. Maybe she was dying.

I ran up the stairs two at a time. Tom pounded up behind me.

At the top of the stairs I heard her crying. I could hear the soft murmur of Daddy's voice. The sounds were coming from my room.

After all the noise I made coming into the house, I tiptoed toward my room. I could tell by Momma's voice that things were not right. I looked in.

Daddy was sitting on my bed. Momma was sitting on her knees on the floor. Piled all around her were boxes. Some were empty. Others were full. Full of Kelly's things. Kelly's stuffed animals. Her clothes. Her shoes and books and drawings and posters and games. Kelly's bed was stripped of its sheets and blankets. The closet door was ajar, and I could see that all the things that had hung there before were gone. Momma was crying. She was wiping her nose with the tail of one of Daddy's work shirts, one that she was wearing, and cradling an old picture of Kelly and me when we were just babies against her chest. It was a picture I had hidden under Kelly's bed long ago. One that I sometimes looked at when I missed Kelly.

"What are you doing?"

I screamed so loudly that Momma and Daddy both jumped. Tom was standing close to me. I could feel his shoulder warm on mine. But I couldn't see him. All I could see was the fury I felt at watching my mother and father pack away my sister's things. Blood was pounding in my ears.

Momma looked at me. Her eyes were swollen and her nose was all red. Her blond hair hung loosely around her shoulders.

"Leah," she said. Momma bowed her head onto the picture she was holding and cried a long, sad wail. "My baby!"

"What are you doing?" I screamed again. I ran into the room and began pulling things out of boxes and held them close and tight to my chest. I kept screaming, "What? What? Why?" I was so angry I thought I could swim to Europe.

"Leah!" said Daddy, and his voice was sharp. He grabbed at my arm, but I was too strong for him. I jerked free, pulling back and stumbling over a box that was already sealed with silver tape. "Goodwill" was marked across it in black Magic Marker. I piled all the things I was holding onto the box and pushed this stuff into the closet, on my hands and knees. Then I crawled on my hands and knees and began throwing things everywhere, in the directions that they should have been. Kelly's blue jeans dress with pink thread—to the closet. Her school books and papers—toward her dresser top. Her cup of pens and pencils—on the bed so I could put them back on the nightstand.

"This is my room," I shouted. "Get out. Both of you. Don't you ever come back in here." I grabbed

Kelly's pillow, naked of its case, and pressed my face into it. Her smell wasn't there.

Daddy watched me openmouthed, and Momma kept on crying.

"Let me alone with what's left of my sister," I shouted.

"Tom," said Daddy, "run home."

"Yes, sir," Tom said. I looked up at my friend. He was crying. He stepped toward me and bent down. He kissed my face. His lips were cool and dry on my cheek. Then he left. The soft patter of his feet echoed in my head. Down the stairs. Through the living room. The door closing with a click.

I turned back to Momma and Daddy. I was ready to start a war.

Momma held up the tiger sweatshirt I'd given Kelly two Christmases ago. I could see the box of Life Savers. Santa looked like he was stuck in the chimney on the wrapping.

"My poor baby," she said, reaching her hands to me, waving me to her with her fingertips. I realized, with a start, that my mother was crying for me.

Suddenly I was crying with her. Great big cries, like bubbles bursting.

"This is all we have of her, Momma," I said, crawling toward her. I nearly fell into her lap. "We can't get rid of this. What will be left?" I covered my face with the sheets from Kelly's bed. "What will be left?"

"We just keep her memories," said Daddy.

"Yeah, right." I laughed, a very unfunny, croaking noise of a laugh. "Even after all this time it just doesn't seem fair," I said.

"It's okay to still hurt," said Daddy. "And it's okay to heal from the hurting. We just need to get rid of some of this stuff. It's like we're waiting for Kelly to come back. And that won't happen. We can't keep living the lie."

"But, Daddy, I can't let it all go. Not to the Goodwill." I was begging him. "Let's just box some of it up. Let's put it in the attic." I was panicky at the thought of losing Kelly's things.

Momma nodded at Daddy and then at me.

Together we sat down and began to go through Kelly's stuff.

Momma let me put the sheets and blankets back on the bed. She let me keep Kelly's "I love you this much" cup and a few other odds and ends. But most of it we packed in boxes. We handed the boxes, one by one, to Daddy so he could put them up in the attic with the Christmas decorations. It seemed right to do that. You know, with the way that Kelly had always felt about Christmas, it just seemed to fit.

September

MOMMA'S NEWS

At first I thought I was dreaming.

About two in the morning Momma came in and sat on my bed. She was humming. She rubbed my feet for a while, until I was good and awake. Then she said real soft, "Leah, we're going to have a baby in March."

"A baby?"

"Yes. I just wanted you to know. I've kept it a secret for a while. I don't know why. I guess I thought you'd be mad at me." She sighed real big, and I lay quiet in the bed, surprised. It was like I had taken a breath and couldn't remember how to let it out again. A baby. After a moment or two Momma started talking.

"I'm not trying to replace Kelly. I don't want you to think that I am. I just want another little baby to love and take care of." Her voice was soft and kind, like my memory of Kelly. Like the feeling growing inside me knowing about my mother. The feeling I had, now, knowing why my father had done so much for his wife. Even the shopping.

"I thought maybe you were dying too," I said.

"No," Momma said. She laughed softly, and it was a clear, happy laugh. "Not for a long time."

"Good," I said. "I mean, I'm glad you're okay. I'm glad you're not . . . you know. And I think I'm glad about this other too." I felt embarrassed that I hadn't known Momma was pregnant.

"I love you, Leah."

"I know," I said. "I love you too."

Momma stood, then padded to the door.

"Wait?" I said.

She turned and looked at me.

"Will you take these for me?" I pulled the box from under my pillow. Momma padded back to my bed and took the Life Savers from my hand. Then she kissed me good-night.

I lay quiet in bed, looking at my room, everything just dark shapes in a night that had no moon.

A baby. A baby. I said the word over and over to myself, softlike.

The word left a feeling in my chest, like a warm breath. The idea would take some getting used to, but the thought of a baby made me sort of happy.

School started on a Wednesday morning. I was up bright and early, dressed, and trying not to remember what had happened the year before. I finally gave up trying to forget Kelly's dying. I sat down on my bed, looked where she had slept, where she would never sleep again, and then I cried.

After a few minutes I went in the bathroom and blew my nose. My face was all splotchy red, but it would be okay by the time I left for school.

Momma was waiting for me in the kitchen. Looking at her closely, I could see her belly starting to get round. She smiled at me from the stove.

"How about some French toast?" she said, and started cooking when I nodded yes.

"It will be a year tomorrow." Momma said this so casually, in between cracking eggs and pouring milk into a bowl, that no outsider would have known she was talking about the death of her very own daughter.

I nodded again, trying not to look where Kelly had fallen that last morning so long ago. Instead I tried to see if I could tell that Momma was pregnant from the back. I couldn't.

"We're going to the cemetery, your Daddy, Papa, and I. I would like for you to come with us." Momma dipped a piece of bread into the egg mixture, then forked the dripping slice into the hot skillet. It sizzled, and Momma looked over at me. "I would like for you to come with us," she said again.

I wondered about the baby. If I thought about it, new in a few months, maybe I *could* go to the cemetery. Maybe this baby meant life would be better for us all. Not so lonely.

"All right, Momma," I said. "I'll go." I didn't want to say yes, but I did for Momma.

Kelly, I thought, would be proud of the way I was doing things that were so hard for me. I mean, it wasn't easy going to see her grave. Or going to school again. It wasn't easy worrying about Vickie, wondering what to do. Kelly, I know, would have thought I was pretty brave. And I guess I was.

Tom was waiting for me on the porch when I walked out after breakfast, letting the screen door slam.

"What are you doing here?" I said, surprised. I was wearing a new pair of blue jeans, some that Daddy had helped me to buy because Momma hadn't been feeling up to it. My old beat-up backpack was over one shoulder. It was empty except for a few spiral notebooks, some yellow pencils, and one big pink eraser.

"I'm riding to school with you." Tom pointed with his chin to his bike, leaning against an old oak tree. He smiled at me and I smiled back. I ran behind my house to get my bicycle.

It was warm, pedaling to school. Tom and I chatted back and forth, about who our new teacher would be and whether we would be able to pick where we wanted to sit or if we'd be placed in alphabetical order.

After we chained our bikes up, I went and waited near the school bus parking lot for Vickie. She got off bus No. 95, and when I saw her, I thought I might throw up. There was a bruise under one eye. It was old and green, and it didn't even look that bad, except I knew how she had gotten it. That's what made me feel so sick. I knew how she had gotten it.

I talked to her like I didn't see her face, like I didn't notice the makeup smoothed over the bruise, like I didn't know who had hurt her. But all day in class, each time I looked at her, I felt my stomach fall. Why had I thought if I ignored what was happening over at Vickie's place, it would go away? Why had I thought Mrs. Abernathy would change? I guess because none of that awful stuff was happening to me.

Mr. Knobloch, our seventh-grade teacher, was wonderful, with lots of fun ideas for writing and science. And he read to us after lunch, even though a few of the boys thought it was silly. But he never seemed to notice Vickie. He never asked her about the mark on her face. And somehow, because he didn't, the day just wasn't as good as it could have been.

October

ADELINE STREET

A few days later, when I could think of nowhere else to turn, I sucked in a big breath and started down the road. I had sworn that I would never go into the Methodist church. And if there hadn't been a change in preachers over at the Baptist church, I would have gotten on my bike and headed on over there. But since I didn't know the preacher at my favorite church anymore and because so much time had passed, I walked the long block down Adeline Street.

It was early Sunday morning, just after the sun had come up, and everything was fresh, including my memories. I knocked on Preacher Johnson's door. After a moment he opened up to me. He looked for a second, and then he said, "You're Sister Orton's child, aren't you?" I nodded. He opened the door wide for me.

I followed him into a room full of heavy, dark furniture and sat in a maroon chair. A wide, shiny desk separated us.

"I—I have a problem," I said.

"And you think I can help?"

"I hope you can." I took a deep breath and told

him everything. I told him about bruises I had noticed on Vickie in school. I told him about that night at her house that seemed especially dark in my memory. I even told him the things Vickie had asked me to keep in confidence. All the while the preacher nodded his head and looked at me with ice blue eyes.

"So that's it," I said when I had told him all I knew. "I'm afraid for her."

Preacher Johnson took a deep breath. "Thank you, Leah," he said after a moment. And then: "I know you haven't exactly liked me."

I felt my face pinken, but I didn't say anything.

"Coming here took a lot of courage. But you've done the right thing." He stood, and I did too. We walked down the long hall, past the main meeting room, to the big outside doors. "Not everything is just in the Lord's hands, you know. He expects us to help our brothers and sisters."

"Does that mean you'll help Vickie?" I said. I had to know he was going to do something for her.

"I'll do all I can," he said. "I promise."

Preacher Johnson held the doors open for me. He watched as I walked toward my house. He was still standing in front of the golden double doors when I looked back. He was like a tiny dark ant, watching.

I stopped under an oak tree, near our big silver mailbox with ORTON painted in large block letters. A mockingbird started singing. A breeze blew in from the ocean. I breathed deep, sniffing the salt air, puffing in an extra breath until it felt like my lungs would pop. For the first time in weeks I was light-shouldered, like I had passed a great big test at school. Talking about Vickie had eased the weight I had been carrying. Things seemed livable now. And good.

I thought about Papa and Tom and Grandma and Uncle Wing, about Momma and Daddy and how much I loved them all. How much they loved me. I thought about the new baby, our new baby, and wondered if it would be a girl. I thought about the preacher saying I had courage. I even thought about Kelly. She would think that I had done the right thing about Vickie, I was sure. I wrapped my arms around myself from the pure pleasure of thinking. I couldn't help but smile at the beauty of it all.

I turned off Adeline Street and ran down the driveway toward my home.